"You're hard to corner."

And he had her well and truly cornered! The wheel turned again, and this time the ride had started, lifting them with a silken rush. The fairgrounds spread out below in a crazy quilt of movement and color.

"Eli's alive, isn't he?" Cameron said.

Meeka looked at him steadily. Cast by the wheel's supporting struts, shadows rippled and fled across his angular face. He had a wonderful mouth, strong, beautifully shaped, with an oddly sensitive quirk to the corners. And she knew already how it felt on hers.

"And you're in on this," Cameron continued, his face hardening when she still didn't speak. He turned to catch the seat beyond her, bracketing her between his arms. "It's been a swindle from day one, hasn't it? A faked letter, a faked death when the going got tough. But how can you look like that and be in on this—" He shook his head angrily. "And knowing that you are, how can I still want to kiss you...?"

Peggy Nicholson, daughter of a Texas wildcatter, comes by her risk-taking naturally. Despite a fear of heights, she has dabbled in rock climbing and has been known to climb scaffolding to repaint her Rhode Island home when needed. She's been a teacher, an artist and a restorer of antique yachts. But her two main passions are sailing and writing, which, she insists, are all the better when combined. As Peggy says, "I can't imagine a nicer way to live."

Books by Peggy Nicholson

HARLEQUIN ROMANCE

3009—TENDER OFFER
3100—BURNING DREAMS
3172—CHECKMATE
3250—PURE AND SIMPLE

HARLEQUIN PRESENTS

732—THE DARLING JADE
741—RUN SO FAR
764—DOLPHINS FOR LUCK

HARLEQUIN SUPERROMANCE

193—SOFT LIES, SUMMER LIGHT
237—CHILD'S PLAY
290—THE LIGHT FANTASTIC

THE TRUTH ABOUT GEORGE

Peggy Nicholson

Harlequin Books

TORONTO • NEW YORK • LONDON
AMSTERDAM • PARIS • SYDNEY • HAMBURG
STOCKHOLM • ATHENS • TOKYO • MILAN
MADRID • WARSAW • BUDAPEST • AUCKLAND

To Zilli, the lion-hearted, surly dachshund, and, with the greatest admiration, to George Washington, true American patriot and true romantic.
(I trust that, ever indulgent of the ladies, George will forgive me this flight of fancy.)

ISBN 0-373-03322-2

THE TRUTH ABOUT GEORGE

This edition published by arrangement with Harlequin Enterprises B. V.

Printed in U.S.A.

CHAPTER ONE

MEEKA STILL MISSED the goose.

Hard to believe, she thought wryly as she watched Eli and his fat dachshund, Zundi, saunter up the drive minus a goose waddling at their heels.

Goose had never taken to Meeka—had been pecking her shoelaces and hissing at her ever since her arrival at Eli's farm eight years ago. And Goose had been a nuisance whenever they went anywhere. He'd been too slow if they went for a walk, and if they drove, he'd wanted the window seat along with Zundi, which left Meeka squinched against Eli, her knees knocking the pickup's gearshift.

So she shouldn't have minded that some speeding driver had turned him into half a pillow's worth of goose down out by the mailbox last month, but... "Doesn't seem the same without you-know-who," she remarked, when Eli dropped onto the porch steps by her feet.

"Shh!" He jerked his chin at Zundi in warning. The goose had come about because Eli, as a joke, had left Zundi alone with a hatching egg. In the way of all geese, the gosling had become "imprinted" on the first living creature it had seen. Like it or not, Zundi had become the de facto mother of the goose, which had followed her from that day onward.

But though Zundi had finally grown resigned to the embarrassment and had ultimately considered the bird a playmate, the dachshund wasn't mourning her feathered child at the moment. Her dark, shiny eyes were fixed on the stack of mail in Eli's lap. She let out a peremptory yelp and sat up—no easy feat for the overweight dog.

"All right, all right, Gezundheit." Eli balanced his reading specs on the end of his long nose, then selected a piece of mail. Zundi flapped her stubby paws as if to hurry him up. "Ad for hearing aids." He snorted—at sixty-three, Eli claimed to have ears like a barn owl—and offered the envelope to the dachshund.

Toppling forward to meet it, she clamped her teeth on it, growled when Eli didn't let go soon enough, then wrenched it out of his grasp. She turned and tore off around the side of the farmhouse.

"Now if you'd just teach her to bury them!" Meeka reminded him with a laugh. Their compost heap had become littered with junk mail since Eli had taught Zundi this latest trick. And naturally it was Meeka who ended up turning the stuff under, along with their kitchen scraps.

"That'll come later." Eli selected a pink envelope and studied its handwritten address, his shaggy brows drawn down. He clicked his tongue and set the letter aside. "Hope she wants to know about some boyfriend," he said, "and not herself. Those *g*'s..."

"Not feeling tactful today?" Meeka teased. Eli made his living, such as it was, analyzing handwriting. Most of his customers were women who'd seen his ads in one of the homemaking or fashion magazines in which he advertised. The usual respondent sent in a sample of a new suitor's penmanship. She wanted to know if he was trustworthy, or generous, or at least not an ax murderer with a mother fixation and a bad credit rating.

"No more than usual."

Meeka smiled to herself and turned back to her sketchbook. Eli possessed all the kindness in the world, and no more tact that a four-year-old. If the emperor were foolish enough to parade past their Vermont farmhouse, Eli would be the first to comment on his new clothes.

Tipping back her head, she studied the pink clematis that twined up a white Doric column to smother the porch's gingerbread trim in a cloud of rosy blooms. It was the perfect subject for a quilt, one she'd been meaning to make for years. She'd use three shades of pink and mauve for the petals, with black swallowtail butterflies flitting from flower to flower. The background would be a grayish blue...

Zundi was back, sitting up and demanding her reward with waving paws. Eli tossed her a biscuit, then, when she'd downed that in a gulp, he handed her another envelope.

"What was that one?" Meeka asked, glancing after the departing dachshund.

"From the government," Eli mumbled as he opened another letter addressed in a feminine hand.

"Not the IRS?" Meeka's voice sharpened with alarm. Several years back, she'd discovered that her uncle had given up paying his income taxes—because in Eli's view, life was short and sweet. He had no patience with anyone who complicated it. So, when the forms had grown too complex for any sensible man, he'd simply stopped bothering.

It had taken an accountant and a lawyer, as well as countless pleading letters from Meeka, before the bureaucrats had been made to see that Eli wasn't a deadbeat, but simply a blithe eccentric. And that the taxes involved weren't worth the trouble of seizing his tiny run-down farm. Finally the Internal Revenue Service had graciously agreed to accept Eli's ninety-eight dollars in back taxes, plus another thousand in interest and penalties. So now they were paying off that debt on the extension plan. "Not the IRS?" she repeated, her heart in her mouth.

"Uh-uh," Eli grunted, reading his letter. "From Senator Talk Much Do Little Tax More. I wrote him last month, said if he was so set on raising taxes, he should consider taxing noise. You'd pay by your decibel output. Chain saws would cost you so much to run, snowmobiles a heck of a lot more...." Eli loathed the noisy wintertime vehicles. "If you ride around in your car with your radio blasting, they tax you. Same for squalling babies in restaurants. We'd pay off the national debt in no time."

"I like it," said Meeka, wondering if he was serious. With Eli, it was often hard to tell. "What did the senator think?"

"Didn't open it to find out," Eli mumbled. "He'll do it or he won't."

Meeka nodded as she sketched in the first butterfly hanging upside down from a blossom. Eli lost interest in most projects as fast as he thought of them—except for his practical jokes, with which he took infinite pains. She'd check out the senator's views herself when she next tossed the compost pile.

Eyes still on his letter, Eli flipped the growling dachshund a treat. "Keep your pants on," he told Zundi when she snarled her demand for another errand. "You don't get this one." He turned the sample over to examine the other side. "This fella might be almost normal. *T*'s are crossed about right. Good *n*'s. He's a little stodgy maybe, but normal."

"She'll be pleased to hear it."

Eli chuckled suddenly and tipped up his long chin to stare at the sky.

"Yes?" Meeka prompted, recognizing a brainstorm when she saw one.

"What if I wrote her back," Eli mused, starting to smile under his snowy white mustache, "and told her that this is really strange. Her sweetheart's a gentleman and a scholar, but she's the ninth woman who's sent me a sample of his writing this month!"

"You'll do no such thing!" Meeka laughed. Eli loved to tease, but in eight years of knowing him, she'd yet to see him choose a vulnerable target. It was the pompous, the know-it-alls, the bureaucrats with their petty tyrannies that aroused his ever-simmering sense of mischief.

"Guess not," Eli agreed with a trace of regret as he reached for his last letter. "Man's writing," he informed

Zundi, who was almost dancing with impatience by now. He tore open the envelope, drew out a folded sheet of paper, and a check fluttered out and landed on the top step.

Meeka picked it up. It was made out to Eli, for the sum of— She blinked, read it again, then swallowed hard. There were too many zeros, more than she'd ever seen on a check. "A hundred thousand dollars!" she croaked, just as Eli laughed aloud.

"That derned fool! He got me!" Eli chuckled delightedly.

"Eli, it's for one hundred—yes, it really is," Meeka babbled, reading the check yet again. "For one hundred thousand!" She lowered it to stare at him, dread dawning. "What did you do?" Because this time, whatever he'd done, she was already certain it wouldn't be so easy to get him out of it.

Eli slapped his knee. "That derned Henry Calloway! I never knew he had it in him! He got me but good!"

"Got you how?" Meeka demanded, shoving the check at him. She didn't want to hold it. It was trouble. But then, it was probably counterfeit. She snatched it back and scrutinized it. But no, it looked all too legal—a cashier's check, issued by a bank in New York City.

"Henry was supposed to help me out with a joke. But derned if he didn't turn it around on me—but good!" Eli laughed and accepted the check with hardly a glance. He tucked it into his shirt pocket. "The joke was supposed to be on Justin Hawthorne."

Justin Hawthorne was their new neighbor—at least new as Vermonters counted residency. He was the owner of the George Washington Inn and founder of the Green Mountain Sons of Liberty, an American Revolution battle-reenactment club.

More to the point, Eli suspected Justin of murdering the goose. An ex-New Yorker, Justin had moved to the country for its peace and quiet, but he'd never settled down to country pace. He was always speeding between his inn and town in quest of bagels, or smoked salmon, or the *New York Times*. And he'd had little patience with a dachshund and goose who thought they owned the narrow country road that wound past Eli's farm and Justin's inn. He'd always had a particularly vicious way of blaring the horn on his silver convertible whenever Zundi and Goose had crossed his path.

Meeka preferred to think the tragedy had been an accident—some lost tourist had taken the bend too fast to brake as Goose had waddled across the road. But Eli was convinced the deed was intentional goose-slaughter and that the culprit was Hawthorne.

And if that wasn't enough excuse for her uncle to target the innkeeper for one of his famous practical jokes, there was the inn itself. Until Hawthorne had bought the property, it had been known as the old Washington Place. "For Joshua Washington and all the silly, cross-eyed, debt-ridden Washingtons who'd lived there before him back to The Flood!" Eli had snorted, the first time he heard what Hawthorne was claiming in those fancy ads he ran in the *New York Times*.

"George Washington never slept there! At least not the General George Washington who fought the war and fathered the country. Big-city stuff and nonsense!"

No doubt it was, but the tourists came in droves to stay there. And Hawthorne had threatened to sue anyone who disputed his thesis. "Can you prove that George Washington didn't sleep here?" was his battle cry, when anyone questioned his claim.

Of course they couldn't. So most of the townsfolk had simply shrugged and humored him. Correcting a historical fib was hardly worth a lawsuit in most people's books. But Eli...

"What was your joke?" Meeka asked grimly.

"Well, since Justin's so hot on George and the American Revolution, I thought it might be fun to do something historical." Eli preened his mustache. "I wrote a letter in George Washington's own handwriting."

Meeka sucked in a breath. She had no doubt Eli could do it. He could do most anything he set his singular mind to, and with his knowledge of graphology... "What did it say?"

"Well, it was sort of long-winded. They were, back in those days. Comes from no TV, to my mind." Eli pulled himself back from that tangent. "It was addressed to General Clinton, the British general in charge of the king's army, at the time George was supposed to be writing this."

"But what did it say?"

"It said that if General Clinton would agree to give George this, that and the other—gold and a pardon and some other stuff—then George would help Benedict Arnold turn over the fort of West Point to the Brits."

"What?!" Meeka yelped. "You made George Washington out to be a traitor?"

Eli nodded cheerfully. "If the Brits had taken West Point, they'd have controlled the whole Hudson River. That would have cut the colonies in half. The revolution would have ended with a *phhht* like a wet match, and we'd be singing 'God Save the Queen.'" He chortled. "I figured that would give ol' Justin a twinge of heartburn or two!"

"It'll get us sued within an inch of our lives, that's what it'll do, if Justin takes your letter seriously!" Meeka fought the urge to thump her head against the nearest porch column. But someone had sent Eli an enormous check, she recalled with a start. "How does Henry Calloway fit into this? What did you mean that he got you?"

Henry Calloway was an old friend of Eli's, an antique scout. He traveled the country like a gypsy, searching out items for various antique dealers who then resold them. Henry had been through town about two weeks back, though Meeka hadn't seen him. She'd been taking a load of her quilts up to an art gallery in Stowe.

"Well, after I went to all that trouble getting George's letter right, I knew better than to hand it to Justin myself. He'd have never believed it," Eli reasoned. "So I asked Henry to take it to him. He was supposed to tell Justin that he'd found the letter tucked away in a secret drawer in some old desk he'd just bought at a flea market."

"But who sent you the check?" Meeka pleaded, brushing a taffy-colored strand of hair from her dark eyebrows.

"Henry. Here, read his letter." Eli settled back against a column. Zundi humped herself seal-like up the steps and jumped into his lap.

Meeka brushed the hair out of her eyes again and read:

Dear Eli,

The more I looked at your George letter, the more I realized it was a work of art. Sure seemed a shame to waste the letter on a stuffed turkey like Justin Hawthorne! I had to drive down to New York, anyway, to bring a buddy of mine a load of dug bottles, so just for the fun of it, I took your letter along. Showed it to the editor of *American Historic* magazine and told him I'd found it in a secret drawer of an old desk, and I didn't know what to make of it. I asked him what he thought.

He didn't say much at first, but I thought he might just swallow his teeth! Then he asked me, real casual-like, if he could show it to a friend of his, who knew a bit about old documents.

Anyway, he did, and the long and the short of it is his expert guy said it looked absolutely authentic. You must have done some job with the ink and the paper and everything, because he tested it all. Then he—the editor—asked me what I'd take for the letter, and he said maybe he could scrape together five thousand for it. (This old rug trader just laughed.)

So anyway, after about two days of waltzing around on the price, I said maybe I better talk with the *New York Times* or *Newsweek,* and see what they thought it was worth, because I was sure tired of arguing. Haven't seen a grown man come that close to crying in years. Finally he gritted his teeth and paid me two hundred thousand.

Seeing how selling it was my idea and I did such a great job of dealing, I trust you'll think that fifty percent is a reasonable commission? Your half is here enclosed.

Meanwhile, I understand *American Historic* is going to print George's letter and a great big article about it. They're doing a rush job—issue should be out by the time you get this.

As for me, I took mine in cash and I'm headed south. Always wanted to see Mexico. Hear they've got some great deals in old furniture down there, and the señoritas... You might consider cashing your share quick, too, Eli. And traveling for a year or so yourself might be healthy.

Meanwhile, guess this joke's on you, and I'll catch you in a couple of years—if I don't settle down with some sweetie south of the border.

Your grateful pal,
Henry

P.S. Eli, best burn this letter.

"I cannot believe it," Meeka said, her voice very very calm. But her heart was starting to race like a car with a stuck throttle. Henry Calloway, that molting, conniving, rug trader! She'd track him to the ends of the earth and snatch him bald—though of course, he was that already.

"It is pretty hard to believe," Eli agreed, his face aglow. "I mean, I took a lot of care with that ink, used the old formula, mixed up iron gallotannic ink so that it was the exact same chemical composition as the ink they used in the 1700s. And I did a lot of experimenting with how to age the ink with heat, and I started with the right paper—end pages from an old book from 'bout that period, but still. . ." He whistled and shook his head. "I fooled a New York City document expert. That's going some!" He thumped Zundi's side, then tugged her ear. "Pulled the wool over their eyes, Gezundheit!"

This went beyond mischief, it went beyond idiocy, it was unforgivable. It was Trouble. Meeka stood. What to do first?

"And here I thought I was fooling ol' Justin. Heck, I guess I'm fooling half the country!" Eli shook his head at the wonder of it. "What do you figure the readership of that magazine—what was it, *American Historic*—would be? You figure a thousand people are reading my letter about now? Ten thousand?"

Meeka shut her eyes, took a shuddering breath, then opened them again. No use screaming, no use scolding, it would just go in one of Eli's hairy ears and out the other. She'd just have to do what she always did—fix it. The first step was to see if George's letter had really come out in the magazine as Henry claimed. Maybe, please God, this was still some sort of a practical joke. As many people as Eli had fooled, Lord knew someone owed *him* a good one. Meanwhile. . . Fishing in her pocket, she found the keys to her ancient station wagon. "Don't go anywhere till I get back, Eli," she warned, glancing over her shoulder.

But it was doubtful he even heard. He was solemnly shaking first the dachshund's right paw, then her left.

Meeka had to drive all the way into Bennington to find a newsstand that carried *American Historic*.

"Oh, yeah," said the clerk when she asked for the issue. "Only got one left. They just came in this morning, but they've been selling like hotcakes." He laid a magazine before her on the counter.

"Oh, no," Meeka crooned, staring down at it. Until this moment, she had not really believed this was happening. But on the magazine's cover was a portrait of General George Washington on horseback, leading a troop of ragged soldiers. His dour, determined face seemed to stare reproachfully into Meeka's eyes. Below his horse's prancing hooves was printed the question, in bright red type, Washington A Traitor?

"Yeah, can you believe it?" snorted the clerk. "Somebody found a letter claims George was trying to throw the Revolution, that he even asked to be made a general in the British Army!" He shook his head in disgust. "They'll say anything about anybody to sell magazines, but George, c'mon! I'd sooner suspect my Aunt Fanny."

He accepted her money for a copy and was still muttering darkly when Meeka turned away.

She found herself facing a rack of *New York Times* newspapers on which, emblazoned in three-inch type, the headline read Washington: Hero Or Traitor? "They're writing about it, too?" She gulped.

"Everybody's gonna be writing about this one," predicted the clerk, taking the change she thrust at him. "It's gonna be like somebody found out Elvis got a sex change and has been happily working as a home economics teacher in Old Grits, Oklahoma, for the past twenty years. Don't matter whether it's true or not. This one is gonna be *news.*"

Back in her car, Meeka propped the paper against the steering wheel and read, uttering small whimpers and hisses of anguish.

The *Times* reported the discovery of the letter and its purchase for a substantial sum by a leading historical magazine. Reports claimed that the document had been verified by unimpeachable experts, that it was indeed written in George's own hand. And the letter itself was said to be utterly damning—would turn America's most cherished chapter of history on its head. George was reported to have offered to sell out his fatherland for gold, a huge grant of land in the Ohio Valley, a full pardon for himself and his family, and a commission in His Majesty's Army—which, the paper went on to note, George was well-known to have coveted since his youth. More would follow as soon as details were known, the article promised. Reporters were attempting to track down the background of the letter.

"No..." Meeka moaned. The reporters of the *New York Times* could be only slightly less omniscient than God. She glanced wildly over her shoulder, saw no newshounds closing in as yet, then snatched up *American Historic*.

A flip through the glossy, beautifully illustrated periodical showed her a reproduction of the letter itself. Rounded letters in a clear old-fashioned script marched across the page with the steady stride of well-drilled soldiers. Her eyes snatched at a phrase here or there...

> Indeed, sir, I must protest that though after three years of arduous struggle we are no closer to Victory, the same might be said of you.... A welcome cessation to the Bitterness and the Strife between Blood Brothers.... For this Service I would require the sum of...

"Oh, Eli, Eli, Eli!" Meeka dropped the magazine and sat, pulling hard on a lock of her hair. So this was really happening, and it was no local joke. It was starting to look like a national disaster.

The disaster escalated when she drove back through Buxton, the nearest town to Eli's farm. John Quincy, manager of Buxton's only bank, saw her idling along Main Street and flagged her down. "What's Eli up to this time?" he demanded, leaning in at her window.

He knew already? Meeka gulped. Word was spreading like wildfire! "Well..."

"Where the devil did Eli get a check for a hundred thousand dollars, and why did he want it cashed in used, unmarked one-dollar bills?" demanded Quincy, clutching her arm.

"You cashed it?" Meeka whispered.

"I couldn't help it! I checked it eight ways from Sunday, knowing Eli. It was good all right. Nothing I could do. But I darn sure didn't give him used one-dollar bills! He had to settle for bigger stuff."

"You cashed it," Meeka repeated. Why would Eli cash it? He cared nothing for money! Quincy was still talking, but she was no longer registering the conversation. With dazed gentleness, she pushed his arm aside. Then she stepped on the gas and raced for the farm.

CHAPTER TWO

MEEKA CHANTED a prayer as the station wagon bumped down the rutted driveway that led in from the road. Eli was no good with money. He spent it, gave it away, carried it in his pockets in crumpled wads that fell to the ground whenever he pulled out his old red bandanna. But surely he couldn't have spent or lost much in the two short hours she'd been gone? She would convert the money back to a check, return it to the editor of *American Historic* along with a letter that explained all and apologized abjectly.

Yes, but what about the other hundred thousand that Henry Calloway's taken off with? her conscience asked. That sum was lost, probably for good. Henry was no doubt blowing it on bullfights and señoritas and antique paregoric bottles at this very moment. Meeka let out a little yowl of despair and rounded the final curve that brought the farmhouse into view.

Two men turned to stare at her from the front porch. Their wide expectant grins faded as she stepped from the car, and they walked down to meet her.

"Seen Eli?" asked Jack Henley. He was the owner of the town's hardware store. Eli had bought his rattletrap pickup from Jack two years ago and was still paying it off.

"We heard he's done real well for himself," added Herb Cordray. "Won the lottery or something?" Herb worked in the post office, but "that's just a temporary job," he'd always claimed. In reality, or at least in Herb's imagination, he was an inventor. He and Eli were always discussing his latest scheme to make a million. Last year it had been a motorized bowling ball for elderly bowlers who needed extra horsepower to roll a strike. "We knocked, but he ain't answering."

"I guess he's not back yet," she said with a sinking heart. He wasn't inside because Zundi wasn't barking from the windows. The dachshund was fiercely territorial; she went for any unauthorized person or beast that ventured onto the property. Goose and she had made quite the attack team. "Is there anything I can help you with?" she added.

Herb shook his head. "I just wanted to give Eli first crack at investing in the best idea I ever came up with. This one's a sure winner!" With a wary glance at Henley, he took Meeka's arm and tugged her out of earshot. "It's a butterfly caller—like a duck caller, only it's for butterflies," he hissed. "I'm sure they respond to frequencies of sound we can't hear—I just have to do some experiments to figure out which ones. If Eli could help me finance the electronics..."

His grip on her arm tightened when she shook her head. "He'd love this idea, Meeka! I even got the idea from Eli, when he got all the dogs to attend town meeting last year with that silent dog whistle of his."

"I'm sure he'd love it," Meeka said sincerely, "but he's not going to have the money to help you."

"At least he better not throw it away on loony-tune ideas till he's paid his debts!" grumbled Jack Henley, looming up behind them. "If Eli's got money, then I want the rest of what he owes me for that truck."

"Who're you calling loony-tune?" Herb bristled. "You think it's crazy to have original ideas? You think they didn't call Thomas Edison and Einstein crazy? Why, when I've finally made it..."

Meeka wheeled and scampered up the walk to the porch, ran up the steps to the front door, dashed through it and locked it behind her. "Whew!" she said softly, then, "Eli?"

though she knew he wasn't there. But perhaps he'd left her a note. Automatically she headed for the kitchen, the heart of their household.

But no note waited for her on the ancient pine table. Biting her lip, Meeka swung away, then blinked. Eli's battered black rotary phone was off the hook. The receiver dangled over the counter to rest on the cracked tiles of the floor.

Strange.

Stooping to collect it, she hung it up.

She turned away, then spun back as the phone rang. "Hello?" she cried into its mouthpiece. It would be Eli, of course.

"Good afternoon," said a brisk male voice. "This is Peterson of the *New York Times*. May I speak to Mr. Eli Trout, please?"

"Ahh..." Meeka intoned, her mind whirling uselessly in neutral. The *New York Times*. Already. "Er, he's not here right now."

"Then perhaps you could tell me, is your Eli Trout the same Eli Trout who sold the George Washington letter to *American Historic* magazine?" pressed the reporter.

Admit nothing! cried a small instinctive voice. "Er, I don't know anything about that!" she babbled. "You'll have to call back later."

"When do you think—"

She set the phone down. Oh, Lord, how could this be starting so soon? Henry Calloway, she would— Meeka jumped as the phone rang. She marched back to it, lifted the receiver. "Mr. Peterson, I'm sorry, but—"

"Excuse me," said a woman's voice, "but I'm afraid I'm not Mr. Peterson. Is this the Eli Trout residence?"

"Yes, it is," Meeka said grimly.

"Wonderful!" gushed the woman. "I'm calling from the *National Enquirer* and we'd like to know *all* about Mr. Trout! Where did he get that *fascinating* letter? Has it been in the family for ages? I would *love* to do an exclusive interview with—"

"Thank you," Meeka cut in, "but we have no comment at this time. Thanks," she said again as the woman wailed a protest, "but no thanks." She hung up.

A glass of cold water, that was what she needed. Her mouth felt like a desert. She was scared spitless, she realized.

She was opening the refrigerator door when the phone rang for the third time. *Don't answer it,* she told herself. But then, what if it was Eli calling to say he'd bought a hot-air balloon or had gotten a great deal on a boxcar full of whoopee cushions? Meeka could imagine all the possibilities of Eli on the loose with a hundred thousand dollars. She had to catch up with him, and soon. "Hello?" she ventured.

This time it was a reporter from *Newsweek.* The next caller was *Time* magazine. And the caller after that was an unspeakably pushy man from some TV talk show, offering unbelievable money for an exclusive interview. Meeka slammed down the phone and glared at it.

Incredibly, this time it stayed silent.

She heaved a wary sigh, then, watching it as she would have a cornered snake, backed a step toward the door. The question that everyone wanted to know, herself included, was where was Eli? First she had to make sure he wasn't hiding out back in his workshop in the barn. She put a hand on the knob of the back door, then winced as the phone trilled.

Three long strides brought her back across the kitchen. "Hello?"

"This is Cameron Benson," a deep male voice snapped in reply. "I want to speak with Eli Trout."

"You and the rest of the world!" Meeka snapped back. "Take a ticket and stand in line, mister."

"And just who is this?" he demanded.

As if she was the intruder in this kitchen, and this reporter the one whose peace of mind had been blown to the four winds! "I'm Mr. Trout's social secretary," she growled, "but not for long. In fact, I quit. 'Bye now." And she hung up, cutting off a command in midsentence.

The phone rang the instant she put the receiver down. "Arrggh!" She picked it up again, then smacked the disconnect button. Leaving the receiver on its side on the counter, she stormed out the back door.

But Eli wasn't hiding in his workshop. And his pickup wasn't parked in the barn beside his beloved mountain bike. That meant he must still be in town. Probably treating every child he could find to banana splits at Jones' Drugstore. Meeka debated driving back to find him, but the thought of ice cream had set off her stomach. She'd been about to fix lunch, she recalled, when Eli had opened the letter that had started this nightmare. It was now time for dinner. Perhaps a peanut-butter-and-honey sandwich would help her feel more able to cope.

She ate her sandwich while pacing the kitchen and was just downing a glass of milk when a bell rang. She cocked her head as it rang again, then realized it was the doorbell—none of their friends ever used it. Her heart starting a dull thumping progression up her throat, she dashed for the front door.

Eli had bought a Harley and joined the Hell's Angels—had spun out on the highway, and now they were bringing his body home for a proper Hell's Angels wake. Or he'd decided to raise potbelly pigs, and this was the UPS man with a truckload of porkers, or... Meeka swung the door open and found herself blinking at a broad chest clad in a blue cotton workshirt.

With dreamlike reluctance her eyes traveled upward, cataloging a determined jaw—not the least bit softened by a good week's worth of dark beard. A clean-cut, unsmiling mouth. Cheek muscles that seemed to bunch and jump even as she noted that danger signal. An uncompromisingly hawklike nose and, above all, a pair of narrowed amber eyes. "Cameron Benson to see Eli Trout," the apparition said as their gazes met. His voice went with the rest of him—hard, dangerous, tautly controlled.

Somehow she'd thought a reporter would be shorter, weedier, with city-pale skin and a weak chin. Certainly not dressed as if he'd just stepped off the plane from Nairobi. And—she sucked in a startled breath as his hand came up to rest on the doorjamb beside her face—would a reporter smell like this? He smelled not ripe, but richly masculine, as if he'd been sweating in the sun all day, haying or digging a ditch. Not a hint of cologne to him—just the solid, uncompromising aura of a real man.

"I take it you're the social secretary?" he growled when she didn't speak. "Recently resigned, that is?"

That was where she'd heard the name—he was one of the ones who'd called! But she'd assumed he was calling from New York, not from just down the road. His hand was very large, the wrist a marvelous structure of tendons and bone, blurred by the curling dark hairs that swirled across it. His sleeves were rolled up his muscular forearms. She had to stop staring at his arm, though that was easier than looking him in the eye.

"Where is he?" demanded the reporter.

"I don't know." And wouldn't tell him if she did. Meeka squared her shoulders, resenting his tone, the way he towered over her, the impact he had on her. All her instincts screamed for her to shut the door. A good three inches of oak between them, then maybe she could breath again.

"When did you see him last? And who the hell are you? Mrs. Trout?"

That provoked a startled smile from her even as she started to close the door. But her smile vanished when he wedged a foot against the doorjamb. "Wait just a minute," he continued levelly. "We have to talk."

Her chin tipped up as she tightened her grip on the door. "Who says we do? I've been telling you and all the other reporters, no comment, and that's just what it means. I have absolutely nothing to say to you."

"Other reporters?" He shot a scowling glance over his shoulder, then swung back. "They're here already?"

"No, but they've been ringing the phone off the wall." She looked pointedly down at his foot. It was clad in a big leather boot, so stained and scuffed he might have tramped from New York City to Vermont in it.

He made a sound deep in his throat—it would likely have been a curse had he let it out. "Has he talked to any of them?"

Meeka shrugged. "I have no idea." Nor was it any of his business. "Now if you'll just..." She closed the door another inch. But he didn't budge. His other hand came up to curl around its edge, holding it open.

"I'm afraid I won't," he said, his voice somehow sounding more dangerous as it became softer and almost silkily polite. "Perhaps you didn't catch my name. It's Cameron Benson."

"So?" He was so famous she was supposed to know his name? His ego was as healthy as the rest of him!

"And so I'm the publisher—and owner—of a magazine called *American Historic,*" he explained, deadly calm.

"Oh," said Meeka in a tiny voice, her hand dropping from the door.

He swung it wide instantly and brushed past her. With a yelp of protest, she whirled around, but he was halfway across the room already. "You can't just—" She caught at his arm, then snatched her hand away as she touched his bare flesh. "You can't just walk in here!"

"Can't I?" With Meeka scurrying at his heels, he stalked into the kitchen, swept it with one glance, then yanked a dish towel from its hook by the sink. He wheeled—and she ran smack into him. "Here." Catching her shoulder to steady her, he wiped the towel across her mouth.

"What?!" she sputtered.

"I'm tired of looking at that milk mustache." He scrubbed her lips once more, then dropped the towel in her hands. "Is he upstairs?"

But she was too furious to speak and too busy turning three shades of crimson. He set her aside and strode out of the room. By the time she caught up with him, he was halfway up the stairs.

"You have no right!" she cried, clutching the banister, but unwilling to follow. Her shoulder still tingled where he'd gripped her, and somehow the thought of the bedrooms upstairs—

"Don't I?" he growled, returning to the landing. "I take it he's received his check by now? Is that why he's not here? Has he cut and run?"

That sounded too close to the awful truth. She bit her bottom lip and stared up at him.

"Has he run?" Benson repeated, descending the stairs two at a time. He caught her arm as if she might bolt, as well.

"I don't know." She shrugged. His hand rose with the gesture, and she shivered.

"You're Mrs. Trout?" he guessed, his fingers tensing.

In spite of her fear, she had to smile. "No, I'm Meeka—his . . . his niece. Meeka Ranier."

"And is the letter a forgery, Meeka?" he asked, his voice gone soft as a caress.

He was saying her name that way to soothe her—to trick her, she realized. She jerked her arm free. "Why would you buy a forgery? You paid two hundred thousand for it." The thought made her ill.

"My editor, Peter Drysdale, paid two hundred grand for it—while I was out of the country," Benson snapped. "I wouldn't have paid a red cent for such hogwash."

"Why are you so sure it's hogwash?" she asked, feeling foolish even as she did so. No one knew better than she that it was! But still. "Your experts said it was genuine, didn't they?"

"*One* expert authenticated it," Benson said with a grimace. "That's not enough. And I wouldn't believe it if it was twenty. Not if it was two hundred." Glaring down at her, he propped an elbow on the banister. Slowly, his body slouched toward that support. For a moment he looked more weary than furious.

"Why not?" Meeka asked.

"Because if there was ever a true American hero, it was George Washington," Benson said simply. "George wouldn't have sold out. And that somebody would slander him... that they would use my magazine to ruin his reputation..." His face hardened with his voice, and he jerked upright. "The fraud's bad enough—I've better things to do with my money than to hand it over to a con man. But to tear down a man's name, a man who's not here to defend himself..." His golden eyes met hers bleakly. "I wouldn't forgive that. I won't forget that. Anybody who'd do that, well, he can rot in jail. So I'll ask you again, Meeka, is the letter a forgery?"

Eli had done it this time. He'd crossed the wrong man. Still and all, it wasn't Eli's fault. He hadn't sold the letter. But try to tell that to this man. Cameron Benson plainly wasn't the type to suffer fools, or foolishness, gladly. She'd better say nothing, then talk to a lawyer—fast. "You'd better go," she said, flinching at the scowl this evoked.

"Not till I see him."

"He's not here and I don't know when he'll return." Meeka turned and marched back to the living room. As she'd hoped, Benson followed, if too close for comfort.

"Then where did he go?"

"I haven't a clue." Eli had always had the catlike talent of vanishing when trouble hit, then sauntering out, smiling, once it had blown by. Perhaps that was what he was doing this time. But whatever he was up to, she didn't want him talking with Benson till she'd consulted their lawyer. Simple apologies weren't going to mend this fuss. One look at Benson's face told her that.

Benson opened and clenched his large hands. "But he will come back?"

"Eventually." That was certain enough. For as if to balance his wayward spirit, Eli was a homebody at heart. He'd been born on this farm, had lived here all his life—had seldom strayed far past the town, except for the years when he'd visited Meeka's mother. He was fond of boasting that he'd never left the state of Vermont in his life and that he had no plans to.

"'Eventually' isn't soon enough! I've got to get to him before the others find him."

"I can't help you." Meeka went to the front door, which still stood ajar. "Now if you'll excuse me."

"Oh, no." Benson shook his dark head. "I'm waiting here, Meeka. We're going to get to the bottom of this, and the sooner the better."

Already stretched taut, her nerves frayed like a cable parting its strands one by one. There was no way she'd spend the evening with this furious stranger parked in her living room! With him inside it, the whole house seemed too small. "I'm sorry, but I don't want you here," she said, too frazzled to soften her response.

Benson was past tact, as well. "Tough." He hooked his thumbs in his jeans pockets and seemed to grow another inch. Which made him about six-two, by Meeka's estimate. Much too big to be moved by force.

She drew a shaking breath, then let it out slowly through clenched teeth. "That's fine, Mr. Benson," she said at last. "You make yourself comfortable, then. I'll go next door, call the police and tell them you're trespassing." Perhaps they'd bring a tow truck and haul him away!

His head came up. Eyes narrowing, he started to say something, then thought better of it. His jaw muscles jumped as if he was biting the words back. "That's the way it is, huh?"

With this man that was the way it had to be. She could picture no middle way with him, nothing short of surrender, and she wasn't about to do that. "That's the way it is." She'd been protecting Eli for eight years now, and she wasn't about to stop tonight. Not even for a man like— She shook her head, not sure where that thought had come from, or where it was leading.

"Then I'll wait in my car, if that's acceptable?" he asked with savage courtesy.

It wasn't. She'd be as painfully aware of him in her front yard as she would if he stayed on the couch. But Meeka had pushed him as far as she dared. She shrugged. "Up to you. Eli might not be home for hours."

"I'll wait." Benson paused beside her in the doorway. Looking down at her, he started to add something, then changed his mind. "I'll wait." He closed the door behind him.

He'd been so real, so...so vital, it was hard to believe he was gone. Meeka stood, staring blankly at the door. Closing her eyes, she heaved a sigh of exquisite relief—which ended in a wince when a distant car door slammed.

Eli's done it this time! This time, he really had.

Once she'd recovered, Meeka tried to reach Mr. Finley. The old lawyer had done wonders in helping her save Eli from the tax mess. He was the logical one to call now, especially since he was the only lawyer she knew who'd work on credit.

But though it was nearly dark, Mr. Finley wasn't at home and he'd already left his office. Meeka left a message on his answering machine, asking for an appointment in the morning, then replaced the receiver and sat, chewing her lip. What else could she do? Go hunt for Eli? But Benson's car was blocking the drive. He might back out and let her by, but if he did, he'd surely follow.

She let out a squeak as the phone rang.

"Have you heard from him yet?" demanded Benson's husky growl.

"I thought you were..." Meeka stretched the phone cord till she could peer out the kitchen window. She could just make out the gleam of a dark car, parked in the shadows beneath the lilacs. "You *are* still here. At least your car is. Then how...?"

"Welcome to the nineties, Meeka," he said, sounding wearily amused. "We all have car phones now."

"Not in Vermont, we don't!"

"You wouldn't," he agreed, making it no compliment. "Have you heard from your uncle?"

"No, and I'm going to hang up now." This felt too strange, his low voice tickling her ear, while he sat behind that gleam of glass and chrome not thirty yards away. And come to think of it, with the kitchen light on, he could probably see her at the window. She ducked and was rewarded with a chuckle. "I'm hanging up," she repeated, feeling her cheeks warm for the second time that day. Clearly he thought she was a hick.

"Stay and talk," he countered. "Or better yet, invite me in and make me a cup of coffee and a sandwich."

"Why would I do that?" Feed a man who'd see Eli rot in prison?

"Just fantasizing," he admitted after a moment's silence. "The last real meal I remember was in Bolivia. I guess that was...yesterday."

"What were you doing in Bolivia?" Meeka propped a hip against the kitchen table and closed her eyes. She could hear crickets through the window, hear them coming through the phone, as well. She might have been standing with him somewhere in the dark, no reality but their muted voices, talking about places she'd never even imagined. With a person like none she'd ever imagined.

"Was about to climb a mountain when my secretary finally reached me. She got a ham operator to patch her through to a mining company, about sixty miles down the valley. They contacted a village priest, who sent an Indian kid, who... Anyway, once I heard, I got here fast as I could, though not fast enough to stop the issue. Blew through New York this morning, got the story from Drysdale and kept on moving. So here I am, badly in need of a shave and a cup of coffee."

Meeka ignored the hint. "You talked to your editor?"

"My editor, now on a leave of absence," Benson amended, all the lazy humor leaving his voice. "If I find out the letter's as bogus as I figure it is, he'll be my ex-editor before he can say triple-check-your-sources. How a grown man could have bought a scam like this one..."

Any sympathy Meeka had been feeling vanished. If Benson could fire his own editor, then clearly he'd show no mercy to a stranger like Eli. "You're not even sure it's a scam," she said.

"So prove me wrong, Meeka," he taunted. "Where'd Uncle Eli find the letter?"

"You'll have to ask him." Admit nothing. Surely that was the safest course of action till she'd talked with Mr. Finley.

"Where *is* Uncle Eli? It's past nine and I thought you Vermonters went to bed with the chickens. He's flown the coop, hasn't he, Meeka?"

Fear that he was right only made her angrier. "Good night, Mr. Benson."

"And where are you off to?" he demanded.

"To the shower," she said. Then to bed, if not to sleep.

"Something more to fantasize about," he murmured.

In her mind's eye she could see him smile—could somehow see him seeing her. With a little growl of disgust for giving herself away like that, she slammed down the receiver. Then, remembering, she took it off the hook again and left it there.

Meeka had finished her shower and was just combing out her hair when she heard Zundi bark. And keep on barking.

Dropping her comb, she yanked the sash tight on her old terry cloth robe and pattered barefoot out of the bathroom. If Zundi was back, then so was Eli. She had to get him inside before he met up with Benson. She didn't want him admitting a thing without Finley's say-so.

"Zundi!" she called as she flung open the front door.

The dachshund's outraged clamor continued—Gezundheit had never obeyed anyone but Eli. Her baying was accompanied by a scrabbling sound, and Meeka could just make out the dark shape of the dog. Reared up against the driver's door, Zundi was clawing at the paint—of a shiny black Jaguar.

"Cut that out!" Benson commanded from his open window. "Get down, or it's bun-and-mustard time."

At the insult, Zundi snarled and leapt toward his voice. She fell back, her claws screeching across the metal. She bounced up again and yelped louder, punctuating her barks with futile, short-legged hops.

"Stop that!" hollered Benson. "Down!"

"Gezundheit!" Meeka cried, hurrying across the lawn.

"She's not sneezing, lady. She's wrecking my paint job. Down!"

"Gezundheit! Here, girl!"

Ignoring her, the dachshund scrabbled frantically at the Jaguar's door.

"Get!" Benson swatted at the dog with something dark. "Get out of here, you overweight, pyschotic—"

"Don't!" Meeka cried, but Zundi could take care of herself. With a snarl, the dachshund latched onto his weapon, hung all her weight on it and wrenched it free.

"My hat! That does it!" Benson's voice had gone almost polite—a very bad sign.

"Don't get out of the car!" Meeka warned. She dashed after the dachshund, then lost her as Zundi ducked behind a front wheel.

But Benson took orders about as well as the dog. His door clicked and he stepped out stiffly and stood, then jumped violently. "Damn!"

The growl of a dog with its mouth full of pants cuff made it clear what had happened—Zundi was attacking from beneath the car.

"By God, that's enough of— *Damn*!" A metallic crack sounded as some portion of the publisher's anatomy—most likely an elbow—made contact with the car's side.

Zundi's worrying snarl took on a note of triumph. She knew when the prey was weakening.

"Zundi!" Meeka yelled, giggling too hard to hide it.

The dachshund was out in the open now, trying to drag Benson down the drive by his pants cuff. Her claws digging into the dirt, she humped herself backward, shaking her head and growling.

"Get her off me, Meeka, or so help me..." He lifted his assaulted leg in the air. The dachshund dangled, writhing and still growling, then dropped—and jumped for his other leg.

"That does it!" Benson drew back his boot.

"No!" Meeka lunged at him from behind, caught him in a bear hug and yanked backward.

Standing on one beleaguered foot, Benson didn't stand a chance. "Hey!" He tilted, then toppled hard, twisting away from Meeka as they fell.

They landed in the grass by the car, Meeka still hugging him, her arm pinned beneath his ribs. She was giggling too hard to draw breath.

Winded himself, Benson was more creative, swearing something about a "sawed-off, bug-eyed, *rabid,* misbegotten, bloated sorry excuse for a frankfurter!" and what he would do once he got his hands on the dog, all the while wriggling around to face Meeka. "And you're no better!" he told her when she laughed in his face. "What the devil did you tackle me for?"

"You were going to kick her!"

"The hell I was! I was considering getting back in the car and running her down, but I do not—most emphatically—kick mutts that don't come up to my kneecap. Though I'm thinking of revising that policy." He drew a breath, then let it out in a growl. "What's so damned funny?"

Nose to nose with him, she didn't dare say it, but then couldn't contain herself. "Y-you." That set her off again.

He snarled something under his breath and lay there, staring at her. Then, slowly, his hand rose to lift a lock of damp hair off her cheek. "Where the hell did the hell-hound go?" he demanded. "She's missing her chance to go for my throat."

Meeka stopped giggling to listen. She thought she caught the distant clicking of the dachshund's paws on the gravel drive, then there was nothing but the sound of crickets. "Sh-she's gone." Which meant Eli had called her off with his silent whistle. Otherwise Zundi would never have backed down. "Quit" wasn't a word in the dachsund's vocabulary.

"Was that your dog?" Benson propped himself up on one elbow.

"Eli's." Meeka put a hand to her still vibrating stomach. Distantly she heard Eli's old truck start up. He must have parked out by the road and reconnoitered on foot, sending Zundi on ahead. So he knew that he was now the hunted—must have known since this afternoon, when the calls started coming.

"Your uncle's!" Benson bolted upright. "Does that mean..."

"He's gone, too."

"The hell he is!" Benson leapt to his feet. "Was that his car I just heard?"

"Yes, but he's gone now. It's only a mile to town." Eli would find shelter with one of his many friends or he might camp out. He always kept a sleeping bag in the truck.

"What does he drive?"

Meeka stayed silent, then gasped as he stooped, caught her arms and drew her up to a sitting position. "What... does...he...drive, Meeka?" the publisher asked, his voice very very gentle.

She knew better than to stonewall. "A pickup. But you won't catch him now."

"Want to bet?" He lifted her to her feet with an ease that somehow pleased, even as it disturbed her, then glanced around. "My hat."

"Turn your headlights on." She rubbed her arms where he'd held her.

But though they searched the drive around the Jaguar, then moved the car to check the ground beneath, Benson's hat was nowhere to be found.

"Zundi must have taken it," Meeka admitted at last. The dachshund had a fondness for trophies.

"That does it," Benson said, and though he hadn't raised his voice, it was a declaration of war. "I've had that hat since nineteen..." With a wordless growl, he swung into the Jaguar, started it with a roar and zoomed backward down the driveway.

One hand half lifted, Meeka stood in his headlights and watched him go. Though she was laughing inwardly, she was careful not to smile. He was mad enough already.

CHAPTER THREE

MORNING SUNLIGHT turned Mr. Finley's office into a study in red and gold. Walls of red leather-bound books surrounded Meeka, and dust particles spun in the honeyed air. She felt as if she were sitting in the middle of a dusty rose. Perhaps that was because Mr. Finley reminded her of a bumblebee.

Looking round and rather fuzzy in his ancient black suit, he buzzed to himself as he leafed through a legal volume. "Mmmmm..." He turned a page, then shut the volume on his finger. "Hmmm..."

"But he didn't mean to do it," Meeka tried for the third time. "I mean, he didn't mean to do it to this Benson and his magazine. The letter was meant for Justin Hawthorne."

"Best keep that to yourself," Mr. Finley murmured, tilting back in his swivel chair. "Hawthorne would sue his own mother if she looked at him cross-eyed. You don't need any more trouble."

"That's for sure! But since Eli didn't intend to fool Benson..." Her voice faded as Mr. Finley fixed her with his tiny shrewd eyes.

"The law's interested in actions, not intentions, Meeka. And I'd say the main action here that will interest a prosecutor is that Eli cashed the check. Even if Eli didn't intend to defraud Benson, he knowingly profited by the fraud. And he's made no move to restore the money."

"But he will, he will, *he will,* just as soon as I catch up with him!"

"Furthermore," Finley intoned, "how can you prove that Eli didn't intend to sell this forgery to *American Historic* from the start? You'd have a hard time convincing a New York City jury that anyone would take such care to produce a perfect forgery simply as a practical joke."

"The letter from Henry Calloway—that explains it all!"

Mr. Finley stroked his bald pate with a single fingertip. "And where's the letter?" he reminded her.

"Eli has it." Or had it yesterday. Meeka slumped back in her chair.

Mr. Finley made a harrumphing sound. After the tax fiasco, he knew Eli's way with paper all too well. By now, Henry Calloway's letter had probably been converted to a paper airplane or an origami crane. Or Eli had drawn a cartoon on the back of it and given it to some child. "So much for that," the lawyer said dryly.

"What are we going to do?" Meeka wailed.

Mr. Finley made a long-drawn-out buzzing sound and wheeled around in his chair to face the window. Meeka clasped her hands till her knuckles ached. He wasn't going to accept that "we"—wasn't going to take the case at all. And she could hardly blame him. She still owed the lawyer three hundred dollars for the tax case. Clearly Eli was a losing proposition.

Slowly Mr. Finley rotated to face her. He sighed and rubbed his shiny head. "Bring him in here, Meeka—with the hundred thousand—and I'll see what I can do. Maybe we can negotiate some sort of settlement."

Oh, thank you! "But what about the other hundred thousand that Henry Calloway took?"

Finley shrugged. "I'll maintain that that's between Benson and Calloway. But if I were Benson, I'd chase the easiest one to catch and dun him for the whole amount."

"But we haven't got it!"

Finley shrugged again. "Then I'm afraid it comes down to how reasonable this Benson is. Is he willing to settle for half, to save himself some time and legal fees? Or is he the type who'll want his pound of flesh even if it costs him ten pounds to collect?"

Meeka bit down on her bottom lip. She had no idea.

"You've got to look at it from the plaintiff's point of view," Finley added. "Even if Eli gave him back all his money today, Benson's been damaged. His magazine has a reputation. If it turns out he's been tricked into publishing a blatant calumny about the father of our country, what does that do to his magazine's credibility?"

"It does it no good," Meeka admitted in a tiny voice.

"So he has grounds for a damage suit—substantial damages." Finley rolled out the last two words with almost sensual pleasure.

"But we've nothing he could take, except the farm," Meeka said. And Benson didn't look like the type to fancy a run-down farmhouse. Not if he drove a Jaguar and enjoyed exotic vacations. More than likely he preferred the penthouse life-style.

"Then it comes down to how vindictive he is," Finley repeated. "He might settle for nothing. He might settle for seeing Eli in jail."

"Please... you're scaring me." Eli in jail—it was unthinkable. Like butterflies in harness or cobwebs spun to order. It would kill him, at least kill the part of him that made him Eli.

"I've been *trying* to scare Eli for years. I warned him that if he kept on like this... But would he listen?"

Meeka shook her head miserably. Eli heard only what he wanted to hear. "So there's no hope?" she said at last.

Finley pursed his lips. "I didn't say that. There's always a chance of a settlement, or..." He swiveled away from her again. "Just how good do you think this forgery really is?"

"How good?" Meeka stared at the pinkening tips of the lawyer's ears. "I don't know. It fooled an expert." Must have dazzled him, to make him buy such an outrageous story. But that wasn't so surprising. When Eli set his mind to something... "Why?"

"I presume that if Benson doesn't believe his own expert, then he's submitting the letter to other authorities. But if the first expert believed it authentic, then just possibly..." Mr. Finley's ears turned a shade rosier.

"The others might think it was genuine, too?" Meeka stared at the lawyer. He *couldn't* be suggesting...

"And if they do—" Mr. Finley rotated once more and met her eyes with cool defiance "—then where's the damage to Benson? He's bought himself the scoop of the century. The publicity for his magazine alone would be worth—"

"But it's not true!" Meeka burst out. "Poor George Washington—he doesn't deserve this! To have people believe he was a traitor?"

Finley sniffed. "Truth is relative. I daresay if we really knew the truth about many historical events that we believe to be factual... Besides, George has gone to his reward. It's Eli..."

...whom we have to save. Meeka closed her eyes. It wasn't fair, wasn't fair to George at all, but then, was it fair that Henry Calloway had placed Eli in this position? "You really think that might happen?"

Finley shrugged. "It's just one possible turn of events. *But?*" He aimed a stubby finger between her eyes. "Because it's a possibility, and because it might well be our last-ditch hope, I cannot emphasize this too strongly. Don't...tell...*anyone* that the letter is a fake. Don't tell any reporters that come asking. Don't tell the police if they ask. Don't tell your best friend. And for *pity's* sake, not a word to Benson! Understood?"

"Yes." Meeka gulped. That was clear enough.

"And the same goes for Eli. Keep him quiet, even if you have to gag him." Mr. Finley flicked an imaginary bit of dust off his skull, adjusted the worn cuffs of his suit, then rose to usher her to the door. "So... go find Eli, bring him to me, and remember, as far as you know, that letter is genuine."

"Right," said Meeka to his closing door. She stood very still, staring at its crazed varnish, then turned and wandered dazedly down the hall to the stairway. *Poor George!*

Take it one step at a time, she reminded herself as she stepped out onto the sidewalk. The first step was to find Eli. She could think of half a dozen households that might have taken him in last night. Perhaps the easiest way to pick up his trail was to stop in at Betsy's Coffee Pot.

Meeka was angling across Main Street when she saw the Jaguar. She stopped in her tracks, turned half-around, then turned back. The sleek black car was parked two blocks down the street. But a quick scan in either direction indicated no sign of Benson. *Could be anywhere.*

Turning back to the diner, she found her eyes homing in on the newspaper box by its entrance. Washington Letter From Vermont! proclaimed the headline of the state's largest newspaper.

The wolves were closing in! With a little moan, Meeka searched the pockets of her denim skirt. She stepped aside as the diner door opened.

"Save your change," said a voice behind her.

"Eep!" Meeka spun to find Cameron Benson standing at her elbow. Grimly ironic, he offered her a folded copy of the same paper.

"Uh, that's okay." On second thought, who needed to read bad news? Meeka drifted backward toward the sidewalk.

Benson closed the distance in a stride. "I stopped by your place an hour ago, but no luck. I take it your uncle never came home?"

"No. No, he didn't." Wherever Benson had spent the night, he had found a razor, since he was now clean-shaven.

A small pale scar angled across his square chin—boyhood fistfight, or a more recent dispute? Whichever, it looked quite at home there. Had she really dared laugh at this man the night before?

"So where is he, Meeka?"

"I don't know. Hey!" she cried as he took her wrist. "What do you—"

"We have to talk," he said, towing her along. "Half the town seems to be watching us from the windows there. Shall we go in and entertain them, or shall we talk in my car?"

Meeka dug in her heels. Benson was overwhelming enough out in the fresh air. "Let them look." She'd be teased for the next month, anyway, what with his holding her hand this way. "And I told you last night, we have nothing to talk about. No comment."

He snorted. "You're going to get mighty bored with saying that. You do realize that every reporter in the country is homing in on this town? By this evening they'll be thicker than locusts."

"I don't understand," she said. "Did Henry tell your editor where to..." Her voice trailed away at the look on Benson's face.

"You know a lot more than you're willing to comment on, don't you?" he said savagely. Clapping an arm around her shoulders, he urged her toward his car again. "No, Calloway didn't give away your uncle's part in this. His story was that he'd bought an old desk from someone up in Vermont. And that he'd found the letter in a hidden drawer in the desk." He looked at her sideways. "But you know that already, don't you?"

She couldn't deny it, felt his arm tense when she didn't.

"But once my fool of an editor paid him off, Calloway took the check straight to our bank in New York," continued Benson. "He broke the check, took his half in cash and had a second cashier's check made out, payable to Eli Trout. Once I learned that, I had my secretary call Vermont Information, and what do you know? They had a listing for an Eli Trout. So here I am."

"And the other reporters?" Meeka leaned back against his arm. They were nearing his car.

His arm tightened automatically, as if she were a lover, rather than a detainee. "We've sprung a leak," he admitted. "It's almost impossible to plug a story this big. They may have traced him through someone at the bank, as I did. Or maybe the first expert Drysdale consulted tipped them off. Or possibly Drysdale himself. Whoever, they'll be here, all right. I'm surprised they're not here already."

"But I don't understand. What do they want?"

He laughed under his breath. "What does a shark want when it smells blood? This is the biggest story in the country, don't you see? They want a piece of it—a piece of your uncle."

"And is that what you want?"

He stopped and swung her to face him, which put them only inches apart. Fighting the urge to brace a hand against his chest, she tipped her head back to meet his angry gaze.

"I want the truth, green eyes. And there are two ways you verify a document of this significance. One is you turn the letter over to the experts—not one expert, but half a dozen of the world's best. That's what Drysdale should have done before he paid out a penny, certainly before he went to print. But he was terrified the story would leak while they were authenticating it and he'd lose his big coup." Benson's fingers moved restlessly along the curve of her shoulder, then stilled abruptly.

"And the other way?" she asked, wondering if she was blushing or if it was just the heat of his body washing against her.

"The other way is you look at the document's provenance. Where did it come from? Whose hands did it pass through? Can it be traced back in a plausible way to the person who supposedly wrote it? That's why I'm here, why every reporter worth his salt in the country will be here any minute."

"But—"

"So don't you see that it makes sense to talk to me first?"

"No, I don't see that." She took a step back.

Instead of freeing her, he simply followed, as if they were dancing a tango. "You're in on this," he said, scowling down at her. "Is this the first scam you and your uncle have pulled, or is this how you make your living?"

Meeka didn't even dignify his assumption with a reply. She took another step back, but again he followed. "Would you mind letting me go?"

"Oh, I'd mind a lot. Is Eli with Henry Calloway?"

"No!" Meeka's rear touched the side of the Jaguar and she let out a yip of surprise. "He isn't, but why don't you go chase Henry? He started it all."

Benson let her go—only to bracket her with his arms. Leaning against his car, he stared down at her. "Talk to me about Henry," he said intensely. "Where has he skipped off to? I've put a detective on his trail, but we've got nothing so far. He hasn't been back to his trailer in Burlington for weeks. But the neighbors say that's his usual pattern."

"It is. He drives all over the country scouting for antiques."

"So he's really a dealer? That much wasn't a lie?"

Meeka nodded and drew a shivering breath. If he didn't let her go soon, she was going to explode. His nearness seemed to rasp at her flesh and she didn't know where to fix her eyes—on his lips, the strong tanned column of his neck, the V of his shirt and the spray of dark hairs it framed. Or on the golden eyes that drilled into her.

"A fact at last!" Benson purred. "And where is Calloway?"

Her eyes shot back up to his. Mr. Finley hadn't told her what to say about Henry. On the one hand, Henry had brought this disaster down on their heads—she saw no need to shelter him. On the other hand, she could see no way to blame him without implicating Eli.

"You *are* in on this!" Benson said bitterly. "What's your cut? Half your uncle's share? A quarter?"

She'd had enough! Meeka set her hands flat on his chest and almost flinched at the hard, warm feel of him. *Enough!* Bracing herself against the car, she started to straighten her arms—

"Meeka?" said a woman's voice. A frizzy red head popped into sight as Irma Hatrick peeped around Benson's broad shoulder. "Excuse me?" The reporter for the *Buxton Daily,* the town paper, sidled around to get a better view. Her bright goggle eyes moved from the position of Meeka's hands to her scarlet cheeks to Benson's face. "Oh, am I interrupting something?"

"Not at all," Benson said pleasantly, as Meeka snatched her hands from his body.

But she couldn't just suspend her hands in midair, and now there didn't seem to be room for them at her sides. She rested them on Benson's forearms, snatched them from there, then crossed her arms awkwardly under her breasts. Seeing him smirk, she gritted her teeth.

"I'm so sorry to interrupt," simpered the reporter, "but Meeka, I'm getting the strangest calls! Three newspapers and a magazine have called the office so far. They want me to cover a story for them. They all say that Eli knows something about this horrible George Washington letter."

"They do?"

"Yes! I tried calling you last night, but your phone was off the hook. And no one's answering this morning. Is Eli home?"

"Er, I d-don't think so," Meeka stammered.

"Then where is he?" Irma asked reasonably.

Benson was starting to look like the cat who'd eaten the canary. "You're not going to answer the lady?" he inquired.

"Irma. Irma Hatrick," Irma supplied.

"You're not going to answer Irma?" Benson coaxed in a velvety voice.

"Hello there!" called a brisk male voice. Meeka turned to find a car stopped alongside the Jaguar. Men leaned from every window, but she didn't know a single one of them. And by their dress, they weren't locals. "We're looking for a Mr. Eli Trout. Could you tell us where—"

"Why, I'm just looking for Eli myself!" caroled Irma, hurrying toward the curb. "Are you gentlemen reporters, by any chance?"

"That's right, ma'am." The speaker swung out of the passenger seat. "Bob Johnson of the *Boston Globe,* and this cast of usual suspects is—"

"And you're Cameron Benson of *American Historic*!" crowed one of his colleagues, scrambling out of the car, his eyes fixed on the publisher. "Mr. Benson, what can you tell us about the George Washington letter? And when do you plan to make it available to the public? The experts say that if they can't examine the document itself..."

His voice was drowned out by a rising crescendo of questions. "What's the background on this letter? That's what we want to know!"

"Who's Eli Trout, and is he the original owner of the letter?"

"How can you believe that the father of our country would—"

"If Judas settled for thirty pieces of silver, then do you think two hundred thousand, adjusted for inflation, is about the going rate to sell out America's greatest hero, Mr. Benson—"

"Have you been in contact with this Trout, or are you here for the same reason we—"

Benson released Meeka and backed away from her, the reporters following him in an elbowing, yelping mass. Meeka stood paralyzed. But Benson shot her a vicious glance over the heads of his interrogators, and that galvanized her into action.

Time to get out of here!

"Why, there's who you should be interviewing!" Irma shrilled above the male hubbub. She pointed dramatically at Meeka. "This is Eli Trout's niece. Meeka can tell you everything you need to know."

As all eyes swung her way, Meeka stood gaping furiously at Irma. Then, as they started toward her, she let out a yelp of sheer terror and fled across the grass.

"Wait, miss!"

"Come back!"

"Miss, please, the American people want to know if—"

But Meeka was halfway through old Mrs. Jordan's hedge of Peace and Queen Elizabeth roses. With a wrench of her thorn-hooked skirt, she pushed on through, bolted around the gazebo in the side yard, then out of sight. As she wriggled through the gap in the back picket fence—eight years and Mr. Jordan had yet to fix it—she could hear the chorus of reporters rounding the house. But they'd never catch her now. She'd played hide and seek in this town for years. It must have been for some purpose, after all.

Four blocks later Meeka staggered up the back steps to Beth Higgins's wraparound porch. A trellis of moonflowers sheltered one end of it, and she collapsed on the oak swing there, chest heaving, eyes wild and hunted. The smell of mint clung to her—she'd trampled through a bed of it, a few blocks back. "Whew!" she gasped, then ducked low on the cushions as a car came idling down the street.

"She's gotta be around here someplace!" declared a voice with a Brooklyn accent.

"Maybe we should go back and hit on Benson?"

"He's going to be a tough nut to crack. The girl'll be easier."

"Where the heck did she go?"

"And tell me why she ran! I told you this story stinks like an August roadkill."

The car prowled on. So this was what Benson had been warning her about. She tried to picture Eli facing those hard-eyed, insatiable men and failed utterly. Because at heart, Eli was shy. He liked to create situations, then watch in silent delight from the sidelines. No way would he want to be the center of such ravenous attention. It would be like watching a rabbit being pecked to death by ravens. She let out a muffled shriek as the door beside her opened.

"Meeka?" Beth Higgins, Meeka's best friend, stood there, with baby Rachel balanced on one hip. "What in heaven's name are you doing?"

"You wouldn't believe." And she couldn't tell, given Mr. Finley's injunction.

"Try me. Come in and have coffee while I feed Rabbit, here. I was just about to, when I heard the swing creaking."

"I'm afraid it'll have to keep, Beth." The reporters had been heading away from where she'd parked her car. "Give me a rain check?"

Beth raised her eyebrows. "Well... sure. Oh! I have a message for you. Mamie Kopesky called. I was to tell you, if I saw you, that Eli spent the night with her and Jud. And that he's out there now if you need him— What?" She laughed as Meeka leapt up and hugged her and the baby.

"I'll explain it all later," Meeka said, letting them go. She leaned out beyond the trellis and checked both ways—the coast was clear. "See you," she cried over her shoulder, then hit the ground running.

CHAPTER FOUR

MEEKA SPOTTED the reporters twice while she was sneaking back to her parking place. The first time they were turning a corner in the distance. The second time they were stopped on Main Street apparently conferring passionately with another carload of strangers. More reporters? Meeka closed her eyes in despair. Like locusts, Benson had warned her. And where was the publisher, come to think of it? His Jaguar was no longer parked near the bank.

Once the reporters had driven off in opposite directions, she scampered across the road and made it to her own car without being spotted. It seemed the angels were on her side.

But if they were, they deserted her when she took the river road out of town. Glancing in her rearview mirror, she saw a black car slide out from behind a lilac hedge to fall in behind her. Benson! Meeka gritted her teeth. The Kopeskys' farm lay only a mile away in the foothills to the north of the river. There was no way she could lose the publisher between here and there—no way she could lose him if she'd had half the state in which to do it. Her doddering station wagon was no match for his sleek monster.

"Blast!" she muttered, then looked back again and let out a groan. Irma Hatrick's little red sports car was closing fast on the Jaguar, beeping its horn merrily as it came.

And behind her followed the reporters—both cars full. "I do not believe this!" Meeka pounded one fist on the driving wheel, then bit her knuckle.

So what now? Decoy them all past the Kopeskys' farm and pray that Eli's truck wasn't parked where Irma would spot it? Or simply do a U-turn, go home, and try to reach Eli later?

"No," she muttered. The sooner she delivered Eli to Mr. Finley, the better. *Press on regardless, then,* she decided grimly. There was no way Benson or the reporters could actually detain her and Eli, after all. She'd bundle him into her car, then race straight back to Mr. Finley.

Behind her, Irma was still frantically honking her horn. Now she pulled out into the oncoming lane and tried to pass Benson. But the Jaguar swung out to the left and stayed there, blocking her way. Irma's beeping turned to a continuous bray of outrage, but the Jag didn't budge.

"Wonderful!" Meeka moaned. As they swept around the bend in noisy formation, she glanced to her right.

Delbert Henley, Jack's brother and the town's police officer, sat in his patrol car parked on the shoulder of the road, glaring at them as they stormed by.

"Just wonderful!" In her rearview mirror, Meeka could see the patrol car begin to move onto the road, obviously hoping to give pursuit. But the reporters, bringing up the rear, wouldn't give way. Instead, both cars sped up, cutting Delbert off. He had to swing in behind them.

Leading this six-car procession, Meeka turned down the lane to the Kopeskys' dairy farm. Irma still blared her horn, and Delbert had switched on his revolving blue light. Meeka could just imagine what the sight looked like to anyone watching through the Kopeskys' front windows!

Meeka pulled into the yard of the farmhouse, sprang from her car and raced for the front door. Eli's truck was nowhere in sight.

"Meeka, what in the world?" cried Mamie Kopesky, coming out onto the porch. Clutching a dish towel, she peered nearsightedly at the cars parking along her drive.

"Quick! Quick! Inside!" Meeka caught Mamie's plump arm and tried to turn her toward the door.

"But who are all these people? What's going on?"

"I'll explain in a minute! But we've got to get inside!" And lock the door. "Eli—he's still here?"

"Yes, he was just drying the dishes for me when we heard you." Mamie turned around, opened the screen door, peered inside. "Eli? Now where did that silly man—"

"Never mind, let's go inside." But Benson was already bounding up the front steps with Irma panting at his heels. Car doors slammed as the reporters scrambled out of their vehicles. At bay, Meeka turned to face them all, her back braced against the door. "You can't see him!" she cried, as Benson loomed over her.

"He's in there?" demanded the publisher. He caught her shoulders with a gentleness that belied the look on his face.

"And just who are you?" asked Mamie. She leaned over the porch railing to squint down at Irma. "Irma, what's the meaning of this?"

But Irma swung away from the steps. For an instant she pointed like a beagle, her sharp nose sniffing the air. Then she trotted to the side of the house. "There he is!" she shrieked. "Eli Trout, you come back here!"

Meeka and Benson raced as one to the edge of the porch and leaned out to peer around the house. They were in time to see Eli's old pickup come bucketing out of the Kopeskys' red barn. Swinging wide round a black-and-white Guernsey cow, the truck headed up through the rocky back pasture.

"Eli, you've got to answer to the American people!" Irma screamed.

Hanging out Eli's window, long ears flapping in the breeze, Zundi answered her with a contemptuous yap. The pickup settled down into second gear and chugged up a cow trail toward the line of the trees.

"Eli Trout!" bellowed one of the newsmen through cupped hands.

Eli never looked back. But from his window, he waved something brown in a sweeping salute. Then the pickup vanished into the woods.

"My hat!" Benson snarled. "By god, he's got my hat!" He swung Meeka around by her elbow. "Where's he going? Where does that trail come back to a passable road?"

Meeka simply laughed up at him. He looked so indignant she couldn't help it. Still laughing, she shook her head.

"All right." Benson bounded off the porch, spun back to survey the line of mountains above the farm, then dashed for his car.

"Now just a damned minute!" yelled Delbert as the publisher tore past.

But if he heard, he didn't stop. The Jaguar roared around in a hairpin turn and stormed down the drive toward the road. Baying like a pack of hounds, the reporters raced for their cars.

"Wait for me!" yelped Irma. "I know the way, I bet!" She scrambled into her car, taking along one reporter who'd been abandoned by his colleagues, and tore after the pack. Light whirling, Delbert pursued the lot of them. Halfway down the drive, he switched on his siren, but no one pulled over. Clearly these were men on expense accounts.

Meeka stood on the porch shaking her head, while the siren grew fainter and fainter, then at last died away to the north.

"What on earth is going *on*?" whimpered Mamie.

Once she'd soothed Mamie, Meeka drove back to her own place. She could think of nothing else to do for the moment. Benson and his colleagues would not catch Eli, of that she was sure.

Her uncle knew the hills around the town as well as he knew his own workshop. And since he'd acquired his mountain bike with its twenty-one gears last year, he'd really taken to the backwoods. There were abandoned logging roads throughout the Green Mountains. No, Benson would not catch Eli till he came down from the hills.

But come down he would eventually, and when he did, Eli would head for home. So she might as well wait for him there. Hiding her car in the barn, then locking her front and back doors, Meeka hunkered down to wait. And to worry.

Eli had never stirred up a hornet's nest like this before. In spite of his bravado back there at the Kopeskys', he must be terrified. Eli didn't like fusses.

It would be days before he came back, she told herself glumly. He'd camp out somewhere by a creek or in one of the abandoned cemeteries that dotted the countryside. Along with his sleeping bag, he kept a few cans of beans and dog food in the back of his pickup for just that purpose. He'd always had a fondness for sleeping under the stars in the summertime. So this exile wouldn't be a hardship for him and Zundi.

It would be harder on her, waiting here, worrying, knowing that their problems would just balloon day by day until they were faced. She'd never been able to get that concept across to Eli.

Fixing a peanut-butter-and-banana sandwich, Meeka wandered into the living room and switched on the television. It was about time for a forecast. *Pray for no rain,* she told herself, thinking of her truant campers.

But instead of the weather, she found a journalist interviewing a smug-looking man who simply had to be a professor. "I fear that, shocking as it is, the letter cannot necessarily be dismissed on contextual grounds," this tweedy gentleman was saying. "After all, it was George Washington himself who discovered Benedict Arnold's supposed plans for betraying the fort at West Point.

"You see, Washington and Lafayette dropped in unexpectedly for dinner at the Arnold home on their way south from Boston. The accepted version claims that Benedict

Arnold, fearing that his plans for treason had been discovered, panicked. He fled to a British warship in the Hudson River. Poor bewildered George was left with Arnold's beautiful and hysterical young wife, er, on his hands, and nothing warm for supper."

The expert tapped the side of his nose and looked wise. "I've always thought that was *terribly* convenient—for George to be Johnny-on-the-spot, just in time to save the country."

The interviewer leaned forward, apparently fascinated. "So you think that George might have been in cahoots with Benedict Arnold in handing over West Point to the British?"

The expert nodded. "Given this letter, it seems all too likely."

"But apparently something went wrong," surmised the newsman, "since West Point wasn't taken."

"Yes," agreed the historian. "Perhaps the British General—General Clinton—would not meet George's price for betraying his country, and so George backed out of the deal. Or perhaps not. Unless we can discover General Clinton's side of the correspondence, we may never know what happened.

"What *is* known is that early the next morning, a British spy was discovered within miles of the Arnold house with the defense plans for West Point hidden in his boots!

"After that, of course, there was no way the planned betrayal could go forward. Benedict Arnold decided to take his chances with the British. Since that day, his name has become synonymous with traitor."

"And George Washington?" prompted the interviewer.

The expert smirked. "If this letter should prove to be true, then my thesis is that George exhibited some of that steely nerve for which he earned renown at Valley Forge. I think George sat tight and brazened the whole thing out. He pinned all the blame on Benedict Arnold, and on Arnold's pretty Peggy—who was a staunch Tory, by the way. And George gave up his dreams of becoming a brigadier general in the British Army and soldiered on."

"And the rest, as they say, is history!" concluded the interviewer. He turned full face to the camera and beamed. "And now a word from our—"

Meeka gave the off button a vicious jab, and the newsman vanished with a pop. "Oh, George, I'm so sorry!" she whispered, then spun toward the kitchen just as a gentle tapping sounded on the back door.

She hurried across the room, and it came again. *Tap tappa-tap tap...*

Shave and a haircut! she translated, unlocking the door. Laughing, she flung it open. "Eli, how did you..." Her grin faded. A small thin man in a beautifully tailored suit stood on the stoop holding a dove-gray fedora in his hands. "Oh! I thought you were—"

"Riley at your service, ma'am." He gave her an abbreviated but courtly bow. "And you would be Ms. Meeka Ranier?" He held out his hand.

"That's right," she said, shaking it. If this was a reporter, why hadn't he tried the front door? But this man had none of a reporter's brashness, if the ones she'd met so far were typical. "And you're...?"

"I was worried about your Uncle Eli," the little man said gravely. "May I come in?"

"Well, I..." Two days ago, she'd have admitted him without question, then set about learning his business. But now...

"Yes," he said with a disarming smile, "I suppose I can see your poin—" He coughed suddenly. "Why, excuse me!" He coughed again, smothered it, then caught at his throat and went on coughing.

"Are you all right?" Meeka asked.

But he'd drawn forth an immaculate handkerchief and was wheezing into it, his shoulders shaking. He shook his head, unable to speak.

"Here, would something to drink help?" Meeka hurried to pour out a glass of water and turned to find that he was now leaning against her kitchen table, still wheezing. "Here, try this!"

"Thank... you," he gasped, and sipped at the water. "Yes, that's much—very much—better, but I wonder if I might sit for a moment?"

"Of course!" Meeka pulled out a chair for him. He was about fifty, she estimated, though he seemed frail for that age. "Are you all right?"

"Yes. You're very kind." Riley folded his handkerchief and tucked it away in a pocket. He beamed at her, then glanced around the kitchen. "What a charming room!" he said brightly.

Meeka frowned. Now that the fit was over, his voice held no trace of hoarseness. "You were saying you were worried about Eli?"

"Yes, well, he's rather between a rock and a hard place, isn't he?" Riley smiled regretfully. "I understand that there are some serious doubts about the authenticity of the George Washington letter, and if it should turn out to be, er, not genuine... Well, he's dealing with Cameron Benson. That can be... dangerous to one's health."

"What do you mean?" Meeka demanded, dropping into a chair across from him. "And who are you, Mr. Riley?"

"Just Riley, please," he said warmly. "Oh, I didn't explain? I'm a writer for *Scoop.*"

"Oh." Meeka winced. She'd seen *Scoop* often enough at the grocery store checkout. She'd never purchased a copy, but she'd often been amused by its headlines. The tabloid always featured articles about penguins who were really aliens in disguise come to steal Earth's ozone. Or unicycle-riding great-grandmothers who'd just given birth to quintuplet chess geniuses. "Oh," she said again. *Oh, wonderful.*

"Oh, it's not what you think," Riley assured her, his eyes twinkling. "We write some quite scholarly articles, as well as the front-page fluff. That's my department. I'm the resident scholar."

"Oh." Perhaps it was so. He could have been a head librarian for a big-city library or a minister from the Midwest. She managed a smile. "Why do you say Benson is dangerous?" Though she'd sensed that about him, herself, hadn't she? But somehow she'd thought that was something just between the two of them—some antipathy, or strange resonance.

"Well, he has a reputation in the trade for being rather vindictive," Riley replied. "They say he hates—just hates—to be made the fool. So if the letter should turn out to be not written by Washington, if it turns out that Benson has made a chump of himself, paying two hundred thousand dollars to libel the father of our country—"

"But he wasn't the one who bought it!" Meeka found herself protesting. "He was out of the States. His editor was the one who..." Her voice faded as Riley's face crinkled in amusement.

"Now who told you that?" he asked with gentle contempt.

"Benson," Meeka admitted, her rising inflection making it a question.

"Ah..." Riley said with a knowing look. "That's what I mean. He won't even own up to making the purchase decision, will he? He's preparing his cover for a strategic retreat if the letter turns out to be a...mistake."

"Oh." Meeka felt a pang of regret, but had no time to examine it as Riley continued.

"He'd rather lay the blame on his own editor if it turns out he's been the fool. And your Uncle Eli?" Harris moved a forefinger across his throat in a slashing motion. "A charge of fraud, I should think. And believe me, Benson won't settle. He'll pursue it to the bitter end."

"But if he wants his money back, he can have it," Meeka protested. At least Eli's half of it—if Eli hadn't lost it already....

"I'm afraid that's not the point, Meeka," Riley said. Putting a hand on top of her fingers, he gave them a compassionate squeeze, then let her go. "If it turns out that the letter's not genuine, Benson will want *vindication,* not money. In order to justify his own gullibility, he'll have to make Eli out to be a conniving villain, a veritable mastermind of forgery. He'll see your uncle in court and then in prison. That's why I said Eli was in danger from him."

It was even worse than she'd feared. And if Benson sought legal revenge, he'd have big-city lawyers who would blow bumbling old Mr. Finley out of the courtroom. Meeka had no doubt of that. "What will we do?"

"Come to me," Riley said simply, spreading his arms wide. "*Scoop* will protect Eli. I assure you that the legal firm we keep on retainer can more than match any shark Benson hires."

"You'd do that?"

Riley nodded modestly. "That's one of *Scoop*'s functions. We're the protectors of the little guy."

"Why would you do that?"

Riley beamed as if she was his student making an excellent point. "Oh, it pays!" He chuckled. "A David-versus-Goliath story always pays! It's newsworthy, Meeka. That's why we'd help you. You give us Uncle Eli's exclusive story about the letter, told in his own words, and we'll take care of him. Benson's lawyers won't touch a hair on his head, I promise you."

"But don't you care if the letter is true or not?" Poor George, did no one care for the truth except her?

"I'm sure it's true," Riley said smoothly. "But will that keep Eli out of prison if Benson's experts declare it's false?"

Tell no one it's a fake, Meeka reminded herself, fighting an urge to confess everything.

"Besides," Riley went on, "does it really matter anymore? Either way, whether the letter's straight from George Washington, or whether it's an unfortunate...mistake, this story is news. The whole country wants to know the truth about George. And *Scoop* wants to tell it."

"I see," said Meeka, not quite sure she did. But still, she was comforted. If worse came to worst, then perhaps here was the solution. "Well, I'll have to think about it, Mr....um, Riley."

"Very good," the man said, taking the hint and rising. "And in the meantime, I trust you're in communication with your uncle?"

"Well, actually..."

Something glinted in the reporter's pale eyes. "You're not?" He stared dreamily into the distance for a moment. "He wouldn't...wouldn't do anything rash now, would he, Meeka? I mean, apparently he's not very pleased with all this publicity. I'm sure it's fairly traumatic and confusing for an elderly gentleman to be hounded this way."

For an uneasy second she entertained the notion, then thrust it out of her mind. "No," she said firmly. Not if he meant what she thought he meant. "No, Eli's shy, that's all. He hates fusses."

Riley collected his hat, and accompanied her to the door. "Well, I hate to say it, Meeka, but this is going to be the mother of all fusses. A question has been raised about the country's greatest hero. And the fuss isn't going to stop until the public's thirst for the truth has been satisfied. You do understand that? The sooner we satisfy America, the sooner the fuss will be over, and we can get back to normal."

That was all she wanted, too. All, she was sure, Eli wanted. As if to underline the futility of that wish, someone rapped on the front door. Meeka winced. To be besieged in her own house. It was a nightmare!

"Well," Riley observed with gentle irony, "your public awaits." He drew out a richly burnished wallet and pulled a card from it. "If you care to reach me, my answering service will know where I am."

"Thank you," Meeka said, and glanced toward the front door, where the knocking had become a determined thumping.

Riley stepped out the back door, then turned on the stoop to smile up at her. "And remember, Meeka. *Scoop* will be honored to save your uncle, but in return, he must give us his exclusive story. My editor demands that, I'm afraid. So contact me the moment you hear from him."

"Thank you," Meeka said, making no promises. She closed the back door, then, squaring her shoulders, headed for the front door, where the thumping had escalated to pounding—the idiot would break it if he didn't stop.

Eli might not do anything desperate, she thought, clenching her teeth, but *she* might. For starters, whoever the obnoxious news hound on the front porch might prove to be, she intended to throw him off her property. "That's enough!" she barked, wrenching open the front door in midthump.

Fist upraised, Cameron Benson stood glowering in her doorway.

CHAPTER FIVE

"OH," SAID MEEKA, starting to close the door.

"Don't even think it," said Benson, catching her wrist. "We're talking—or at least, you're listening." He pulled her across the porch to the steps, and sat down on the top one. "Sit."

Meeka scowled at him, but he simply glared back. She looked down pointedly at his hand and realized, with a shock in the pit of her stomach, how big he was compared to her. The tiniest thrill of fear whispered down her backbone, stirred the hairs at the nape of her neck. Dangerous, Riley had said. Benson certainly looked dangerous at the moment.

"Sit," he repeated with a downward tug.

She sat—as far from him as his reach would permit.

Though he'd shaved that morning, his beard was already shadowing his upper lip and his angular jaw. Perhaps that was what gave him his...uncivilized air, though that of course was ridiculous. Anyone who published a serious historical magazine for a living had to be eminently civilized.

"This isn't working for either of us," Benson said, and let her go.

"What do you mean?" she asked, rubbing his touch from her wrist.

"I mean that I have to get to the truth of the matter—for better or worse—as soon as possible. For everybody's sake. This is bad for the country, bad for my magazine—"

Not necessarily in that order! she thought wryly.

"—and disastrous for George's reputation," Benson continued. "And it can't be good for you or your uncle, either, being trapped in the middle of this media blitzkrieg. We've got to finish this."

"How?" she asked, meeting his gaze.

His gold-brown eyes blazed with intensity. "Let's cut a deal. You bring your uncle in from the hills and bring every last cent of the money he was paid for this forgery..."

"And you'll do what?" Meeka asked, tilting her chin up.

"I'll talk with him," Benson said in a take-no-prisoners voice.

"And then?" Meeka prodded.

"I'll expect him to write out a full confession, which of course I'll publish in my next issue."

"And what else?"

"Then I'll decide whether to bring charges against him or not."

"You call that a deal?" she burst out. It all depended on his mercy, and Riley had said he'd have none.

"It's the only deal I'm planning to offer," he said. "And I'm not offering it for long. In fact—" he glanced at his watch "—you've got exactly five minutes to make up your mind. I'm heartily sick of this nonsense."

Five minutes. Meeka swallowed. Her first impulse was to reject his deal out of hand. Because in return for Eli's surrender, Benson was offering nothing, really. Only the slimmest chance that he'd refrain from prosecuting. On the other hand...

Benson glanced at his watch. "Three minutes, Meeka, my dear."

"I'm not your dear!" she snapped, and brushed her hair out of her eyes. Her head was starting to ache. On the other hand...

"No," he agreed, with the faintest of smiles. "You're not...yet," he added under his breath.

Had he really said what she thought he'd said? Meeka felt her eyes widen. She opened her mouth, then closed it again.

"But I'll 'dear' you from here to Havana if you'll just bring him in," Benson added smoothly.

Meeka studied the gleam in his eyes, uncertain what to say, and quite certain she'd make a fool of herself if she said anything at all. She wanted badly to look away from him, but seemed unable to do so. "I don't know where he is," she said finally, and tucked a strand of hair behind her ear.

His eyes followed the movement. "I don't believe you."

"Then don't believe it!" she flared, snatching her hand away and hiding her fingers between the folds of her skirt.

His eyes followed that gesture, as well, then lingered on her bare knees. Meeka drew in sharp breath and started to rise.

"You make quilts," Benson noted.

She sat back again. "Yes."

His dark brows tilted. "You don't seem the type."

She smiled. He was picturing log-cabin and wedding-ring patterns, all the old lovely traditional designs. No, they weren't her type. Odd that he should sense that. Then her smile faded. "How did you know?"

"I asked around. I was wondering what you did for a living. If you'd had some special need for money recently...."

Meeka bounced to her feet. So he was still working on the theory that she was a junior forger, Eli's accomplice in defrauding his magazine. There was no way she could see to convince him otherwise if she couldn't tell him the truth. But there was no reason she had to stand here letting him insult her. She turned on her heel, then stopped as his hand shot out to close on her ankle.

"We're not done yet," he said very politely.

"Oh, I think we are." She could feel her pulse surging at the base of her throat. "I'm very tired of your treating me like some sort of criminal, Mr. Benson." She touched a finger to the hollow between her collarbones, wondered if he could feel that same slamming pulse in her ankle. "You don't even know if that letter is genuine or not."

"It has to be a fake," he said flatly.

"You don't know that," she insisted. "Your own experts—"

"My own expert," he reminded her. "That is, my blasted editor's—"

"Your own expert thinks it's genuine."

"But I'm having more experts examine it—a whole panel full."

"But has even one of them said it's a forgery yet?" she demanded.

"No," he admitted, "but it takes time to do a proper—"

"Then aren't you getting just a *bit* ahead of yourself, chasing my uncle, demanding your money back, treating me like a...a common thief when, for all you know, you've bought yourself the find of the century?"

His fingers opened gradually, slid from around her, then paused on her Achilles tendon. As if they'd found some mystery that needed solving, they traced up its sensitive length a few inches, then fell away when she stepped out of his reach. "I don't...that is..." He turned toward the driveway, where Irma Hatrick's red sports car was jouncing up the drive.

The reporter wriggled out of her car and came trotting toward them. "My, I always seem to find you two together!" she burbled.

Meeka counted slowly to ten. She'd always suspected that Irma was at heart a thwarted gossip columnist. But though the *Buxton Daily* was too small to support such a feature, that had never stopped Irma. She simply wove threads of gossip into the fabric of her hard-news copy.

"So you do," Benson said noncommittally. With his reflexive courtesy, he'd risen at her arrival. Now he jammed his hands into the pockets of his jeans and turned to study the clematis on the column beside him.

"We're doing a story on Eli for tomorrow's edition," Irma explained to Meeka. "And I wondered if you'd have any comment for the record?"

Benson tipped up his head to inspect the blossoms that draped between the columns. Something about the movement, the rugged line of his throat and shoulder, made Meeka suck in a breath. She forced her attention back to Irma. "What?"

Irma pulled a scrap of paper from her skirt pocket. "Our headline will read George Was Framed!" she said, passing the paper to Meeka.

The subheadline was Local Man Charged With Historical Fraud!

"That's the basic story." Irma pulled a notepad from her pocket and a pencil from behind her ear. "Do you have any comments?"

The paper crackled as Meeka crushed it to a ball. "Just one comment, Irma—you can't print that. You've no proof of that. It's a groundless, baseless, *low* accusation and you know it."

"Wait! Wait! You're going too fast!" Irma cried, scribbling frantically.

Without looking at him, Meeka surrendered the wad to Benson. "I said, print that and with Mr. Finley's help I'll sue you from here to...to Havana." From the corner of her eye, she saw Benson smile, then his smile faded as he smoothed out the paper and read it. "You've no proof of that," she continued. "No proof that Eli's involved in any way, much less that the letter's a fraud! You can't print groundless accusations. You'll scare Eli half to death if he sees this!"

"It most certainly, absolutely, most definitely is *not* groundless!" Irma protested. "Why, the information comes from your gentleman friend here, the man who was defrauded! Ask him, if you don't believe me."

Benson put up his hands as Meeka wheeled on him. "Wait a minute!"

"Did you give them that story?" she blazed.

"Let's discuss this in private, shall we?" Benson slewed a glance at Irma, who was scratching in her notepad again.

"Did you?" she repeated, too outraged to heed the warning.

"He did!" insisted Irma. "That is, he did indirectly."

"Then who told you that directly?" Meeka cried, wanting to snatch the silly notepad and toss it into the compost heap.

Irma drew herself up. "A reporter never reveals her sources."

"Fine. Then you can take your sources, Irma, stick them in your ear and drive them and that red tin can off my property!" Meeka pointed the way.

"This is Eli's property," Irma retorted, retreating anyway.

"You get off Eli's property then, and you better not print that!" Meeka stood, arms folded and eyes glaring, till Irma flounced to her car. Then she turned on Benson. "You gave Irma that story?"

"No, I spoke with the police—Officer Henley—when he stopped me on the road this morning. He was trying to arrest me for resisting arrest, or some such idiocy, so I simply explained to him why I was after your blasted Eli." The publisher set a finger to her lips when she tried to speak. "And I told him in strictest confidence, Meeka."

She threw off his hand. "Strictest confidence! Delbert Henley couldn't keep a secret if he was alone on a desert island! Why, if he was running around on his own wife, she'd be the first to know—he'd tell her himself! *Confidence*—ha!"

"Well, how was I to know that no one in this screwy town has an ounce of professional sense or pride?" Benson demanded.

"Oh, yes, you do things better in New York City, I'm sure!" *Like publish forgeries without checking their authenticity,* she nearly said, then thought better of it. "Just what exactly did you tell Delbert?"

Benson looked uncomfortable. "I told him that the letter was a forgery and that I planned to charge your uncle with fraud."

"I can't believe you did that!" she said, wanting to shake him, though it would have taken three of her to do a proper job of it.

"I wanted Henley to help me find your uncle, not get in my way. That seemed the simplest way to get his cooperation. And odds are I *will* be charging your uncle with fraud, just as soon as—"

"As soon as you know it's a fraud!" she said contemptuously.

Benson's face hardened. "I do know it. George would never—"

"Oh, spare me your George!" she cried. "If you want a 'never,' chew on this one. Eli will never come in to talk with you if he reads that story. He'd never go to jail—not ever. He can't sit still in a room for half an hour. Jail would kill him."

"He should have thought about that before he tried something like this," Benson retorted.

"He didn't..." Frustrated, she shook her head, then hooked a thumb toward the road. "Get out of here, Mr. Benson."

"About our deal..."

She shook her head till her hair whipped her cheeks and kept on pointing. "*No* deal. And if you don't want to be sued within an inch of your sweet life for calling my uncle a forger, you'd better tell Irma to stop the presses." Not that Finley would take such a case on, but it sounded good.

Still, she was surprised when the threat routed him. His jaw knotted, his eyes narrowed, but he nodded shortly and turned to leave. "I'll see what I can do," he growled over his shoulder as he headed for his car.

Watching the publisher's long-legged retreat, she felt like the cartoon character who's been shoving against a very large door—only to fall forward when it's suddenly opened, as if she'd fallen forward on her chin. He moved in a way that hit her the way a wedge of southbound geese, or a late autumn sunset always did. As if something deep within her said, quietly and with absolute conviction, "yes." She shivered and hugged her elbows, shrugging off the sensation. Usually something that had that effect on her became a design for one of her quilts. But how did you put a man on a quilt?

The answer to that was obvious, and she was furious at herself for even thinking that way. Spinning on her heel, she stormed into the house and slammed the door. Then, hating herself for her weakness, she crept to a window and watched him until he was out of sight.

By that evening, the locusts had arrived in earnest. Hoping for an interview with "the mysterious source of the letter that has stunned the nation," a television crew was camped on the front porch. Tripping over their cables and gear were some dozen print reporters, who alternately rapped on her doors and trampled the flower beds, trying to peek past curtains Meeka had drawn at every window.

In spite of all the company, she'd never felt more alone in her life. She wasn't about to go out and face them—she'd tried once, but Benson had been right. For each question to which she answered, "No comment," they simply shouted four more in her face. If they'd even heard her demands that they leave her property, they hadn't heeded them.

And she was cut off by phone, as well. Each time she put the receiver back on its hook and tried to dial out, the phone rang instantly. And each and every caller wanted to know the truth about George.

Finally Meeka retreated to her upstairs bedroom, where she sat huddled on her bed cutting a swath of cotton into squares for a quilt. But with her ears tuned to the thumps and cheerful hard-edged voices of the reporters below on the porch, she'd cut the cloth into smaller and smaller pieces. Ultimately she'd reduced a lovely calico to a pile of useless confetti.

That was the final straw. In a fury, she called the police station.

But Henley was not available. "He's out writing parking tickets," the dispatcher informed her. "He's thinking that if this keeps up, maybe we can buy that new patrol car we need, after all."

"Well, you tell Delbert Henley that if he wants to write tickets, he should come out here and write them!" Meeka raged. "I want every last blasted one of them charged with trespassing!"

"Del said to only bother him for emergencies."

"This is an emergency!"

But when Henley arrived, he was no use at all. "I've been trying to get out here all day," he informed Meeka after he'd elbowed through the crowd, then squeezed through her front door. "I guess Eli ain't back yet?"

When Meeka shook her head, he added, "I've been checking around town and out by the lake, but no sign of him. You can't get him to come in and surrender?"

"Surrender?" Meeka stared at him.

Henley shrugged apologetically. "I'm investigating a case of fraud, Meeka. That's what they pay me to do."

"But...but...has Eli been charged with a crime?" She'd tried to phone Finley off and on all day, but the lawyer was unreachable. He'd always kept erractic office hours in fishing season.

"Not charged, just suspected," Henley said with a judicial air. "But I sure need to question him." He shook his head. "This time he's gone too far, Meeka. That flying-saucer scare at the Labor Day picnic last year was bad enough, but taking on George Washington! Justin Hawthorne's been saying around town that shooting's too good for Eli."

"Justin Hawthorne! Why, if it wasn't for Justin Hawthorne—" Meeka bit her tongue. She'd best leave the innkeeper out of this.

"Don't know why he's so ticked off," added Henley. "Every reporter who comes to town is dying to stay at the George Washington Inn. Hawthorne's making money hand over fist. But he's called a muster of the Green Mountain Sons of Liberty for tomorrow evening. They're going to parade on the green in support of George Washington." Considering that, Henley looked like a cat anticipating canaries. "I'm just about out of parking ticket forms already. These city boys sure believe in double parking."

When he left, the policeman shooed away the hordes. But they surged back as soon as he'd gone.

Surely they'll leave when they get hungry and sleepy, Meeka told herself. *They couldn't stay there all night.*

But she'd underestimated the ingenuity of the members of the American press—they took the night in shifts. And by the next morning, she'd have sworn they'd bred like cockroaches in the dark—there were twice as many on her front steps as there'd been the night before.

By noon Meeka had had enough. She would go mad if she stayed trapped in her own house. And there was no sense in waiting on Eli, either. He'd never return while those vultures perched on his porch.

It took almost an hour of trying before she managed to dial out, but at last she reached Beth Higgins. Beth had always been her friend in need. And better yet, Beth had a very large schoolteacher husband with a sense of humor. "Give me twenty minutes to pack," Meeka told her.

While she waited, she stuffed a few changes of clothes and a pair of pajamas into her backpack. Then she laced her running shoes and spent the rest of the time prowling the house.

When Beth and her husband, Ric, arrived, along with baby Rachel, Meeka heard the stir on the front porch. Lifting her pack, she glided to a curtained front window.

"Who's this?" wondered a reporter aloud.

"Locals," guessed another.

Meeka shrugged on her pack. She didn't dare move the curtain, but with the window raised, she could hear every word.

"Hello!" Beth called briskly from the lawn. "This is Mr. Eli Trout, and I'm his public relations—" Whatever else she'd meant to say was drowned out by the stampede as the reporters charged down the steps.

Meeka twitched the curtain aside and got one glimpse of Beth, Ric and Rachel, surrounded by the mob. Half a dozen microphones were thrust in Ric's face, and his smile already looked a little strained.

No time to lose! She dropped the curtain and sprinted for the back door.

As she'd hoped, all the back-door guards had heard the commotion and abandoned their post. Her heart in her throat, Meeka locked the door behind her, then bolted. Once she'd ducked around the barn, she was home free. Settling into a steady jog, she made the edge of the woods unnoted, then chose the path that headed over the hills toward town.

It was hours later when Ric and Beth returned home. "What's cooking?" Ric demanded, sniffing the air as he walked into the kitchen.

"Strawberry-rhubarb pie," said Meeka, who'd found the ingredients at hand. She'd also washed their breakfast dishes, then drawn a design for a quilt inspired by the blue checked cloth on Beth's table and the African violets on the window ledge beyond.

"You didn't have to do that!" Beth protested, fitting Rachel into her high chair.

"Yes, she did," Ric disagreed. "She'll have to bake me pies for a year to make up for that crew."

"That bad?" Meeka took the pie from the oven.

"I nearly fed one his microphone," Ric grumbled. "And when we told them we'd just been kidding, that I wasn't Eli—"

"They wouldn't believe him till he showed them his driver's license!" Beth giggled. "And then they got mad—even madder when we told them we were just the diversion and meanwhile you'd split."

"They didn't follow you?" Meeka fought the urge to peek out a window.

"That's what kept us so long," Ric explained while he put a knife to the pie. "We took 'em shopping for shoes for Beth over in Bennington. That always bores me silly. I figured it'd bore them, too, and it did. They stuck it out through the first three dozen pairs or so, though."

Beth held up one small foot, neatly shod in a red sandal, and flexed it for Meeka's admiration. "It's an ill wind..." she noted with a grin.

"So tell us what gives," said Ric as he placed a wedge of steaming pie in front of each woman. "Did Eli really forge this George Washington letter?"

"Who told you that?" Meeka hedged, remembering Mr. Finley's instructions.

Ric handed her the newspaper he'd set on the countertop. "That's what the *Buxton Daily* says. They claim Eli's charged with defrauding a magazine for two hundred thousand dollars?"

Meeka stared at the headline and swallowed the lump in her throat. Benson had not quashed the article as he'd promised. So that was what the publisher's word was worth—she'd been right not to trust him. She looked down at her slice of pie, then slid the plate back to Ric. "Better make that a double."

After she'd explained as much as she felt she could to Beth and Ric, Meeka spent the rest of the day phoning friends around town. But no one had seen Eli.

It meant he must still be camping out, which was actually a relief to Meeka. She couldn't imagine what Eli would do, when he saw the headline in the *Daily*.

I have to find him before he reads that and panics, she told herself. Tomorrow, she decided, she'd sneak back to the farm and collect Eli's mountain bike from the barn. She'd ride every hill and trail in the county till she crossed his path.

BUT SHE HAD WORD of Eli long before morning. When the phone rang at eight that evening, Meeka answered, because Ric, Beth and baby Rachel had gone to watch the Green Mountain Sons of Liberty parade on the green.

"Meeka, you wanted to know if we saw Eli," said Iris Estes, the town librarian. "Well, we just passed him, coming back from that silly parade. He was heading the other way when we turned onto our road."

Meeka calculated quickly. There was nothing out that way, except... "You mean he was driving toward the lake?"

"To the lake," Iris confirmed. "We waved him down, but he only stopped for a second."

"What did he say?"

"He just handed Bob that awful hula dancer that's been riding on his dashboard for years—said something about wanting Bob to have it. We didn't pay much notice at the time. I was telling Bob there was no way he'd get me in the car if he put that thing on the dash. And Bob was reaching for it, anyway, when that horrible dog of Eli's leaned out the window and bit him on the thumb! But after Eli'd apologized and driven off and we started to think about it... You don't think he meant... I mean, I never take Eli seriously... But Meeka, he had the funniest look on his face!"

CHAPTER SIX

ELI FREQUENTLY WORE a funny look on his face—that wasn't what terrified her. But giving away his hula dancer! Eli'd sooner part with his life than— "Noooo!" Meeka moaned. There was no reason to panic, she told herself as the car's tires squealed on a curve. No reason at all.

Still, she'd borrowed Beth's car, and if there'd been some way to make the clunker fly... Meeka chose the straightest route to the lake, which took her through the center of town.

A bad mistake, she soon realized. The parade in support of George Washington might be over, but a crowd still mingled on the green and ambled homeward through the streets. Reporters with microphones and notepads scurried hither and yon, waylaying likely targets for person-on-the-street interviews. Traffic was barely creeping, and up ahead...

"Blast!" Meeka swore. Half a block ahead, at the town's only lighted intersection, waited a band of men in American Revolution uniform. Some held burning torches aloft. Others shouldered muskets that looked all too real. They were stopping cars as they reached the intersection. As Meeka watched, a car paused and a tall burly man handed a clipboard in through its open window.

"Justin Hawthorne!" Meeka muttered. The innkeeper was easy to spot. His uniform always looked as if it had come fresh from some colonial dry cleaner's. And Hawthorne carried himself with the pride of a general, even if he was only a self-appointed major two hundred years late for the war.

Reclaiming his petition—at least that was what Meeka supposed it was—Hawthorne gave the driver a snappy salute, then waved him on his way. The Green Mountain Sons of Liberty beckoned the next car forward.

"Aargh!" Meeka groaned. She hadn't time for this! Besides, when Justin reached her car, he wouldn't let her get away with just a signature in support of George Washington, she could be sure of that. As Eli's niece, she'd rate a long-winded harangue at best. At worst, well, Justin probably had some historically correct tar and feathers waiting for anyone who'd dare to insult his commander-in-chief.

Meanwhile Eli... "Oh, please..." She hammered on the steering wheel. Should she turn and go the other way around the green? But the traffic was jammed tight on her bumper, and there were no gaps in the lane of approaching cars, ruling out a U-turn. Suddenly Meeka's eyes focused on the car moving toward her from the opposite direction.

Cameron Benson sat at the wheel of his black Jaguar, his window open and his fingers drumming restlessly on the sleek side of his car.

In another moment he'd be gone. Traffic was moving faster in that direction. With no more thought than that, Meeka switched off her engine, left the keys in the ignition and swung open her door. Someone would park Beth's car to get it out of the way, she had no doubt.

"Wait!" she cried.

The Jaguar jerked to a halt and she dashed in front of its headlights. Benson leaned across to unlock the passenger door and she scrambled inside. "Wait!" she gasped again, as his eyes met hers and his brows lifted ironically. She pointed across the green. "Go that way!"

"Across the grass?" He stared at her. "I've gotten two blasted parking tickets today already, Meeka. You want me to—"

"Eli's gone to the lake!" she said on a half sob. "I've got to get to him!"

"Right." The car rumbled into life, turned and bounced over the curb, then started across the green. "Which way?"

As she pointed, he steered the car past the band shell and down the slope past the duck pond. Behind them a police whistle sounded, people stopped and stared, but Meeka didn't care. "To the right of those fir trees."

Then they were bumping back onto a road and the car accelerated. "Left up ahead, then straight for a while." Houses whipped past, more homeward-bound strollers. A dog ran yelping out from a driveway to snap at their tires, then fell behind. "Turn here."

They bumped over the old red bridge, the river rippling silver below, then it was open road. "Faster! It's been almost half an hour." But Eli wouldn't do anything. This was all a tempest in a teapot, nothing more, surely.

She felt Benson glance at her. "You think—" he began.

"I don't think!" She shook her head fiercely. She wouldn't think it. It couldn't be so. "But he gave away his hula dancer." She put a hand to her mouth, bit savagely at a nail. "And he said once..." He'd said once, when he'd been in one of his fey and philosophical moods, "That... that drowning would be such a nice way to go." Eli had always loved the water.

Benson caught her hand. "Hey, don't be silly!" But the big car's growl rose to a throaty roar, and the overhanging trees swished past like a dark and running river. "He wouldn't..." His fingers tightened on hers. They swept into a curve, then the road straightened out. "How far?"

"Another three miles till we turn."

They covered that three miles at a breathtaking speed, then fishtailed onto the dirt lane that climbed between wooded hills. When they bucked over the last rise, the lake could be seen glimmering in the valley below.

"The parking lot's ahead on the right," she said, a hand at her throat. She tried to laugh. "This is so silly! He's probably not here at all, but . . ." But his truck was, she saw as they bounced into the rutted parking area.

Eli's truck was there and no one else's, though normally there would have been half a dozen cars parked at regular intervals under the trees. But tonight the courting couples must have gone to see the parade.

"This is his truck?" Benson stopped the Jaguar alongside.

"Yes." But no one was in it, she saw at a glance. Which left only the lake. He would be somewhere along the shore, camped for the night. That made the most sense, made the only sense, but why wasn't Zundi barking?

Benson caught her arm as she stumbled down the trail to the beach. "Slow down before you break your neck," he said not unkindly.

"Eli!" she called, tugging forward against his hand. Zundi should be barking by now. "Eli?"

But no one awaited her on the little moon-silvered strip of sand. No one and nothing except for a dark, symmetrical pile near the water's edge. Meeka knelt, touched the pile and felt the softness of fabric.

A light switched on as Benson aimed a flashlight at her discovery. A familiar pair of worn blue jeans with a patch on one knee—a purple calico that Eli had chosen from her scrap bag. He'd folded them neatly.

Meeka let out a hiccuping sob and sat abruptly in the sand. She pulled the jeans onto her lap, and Eli's folded shirt fell to one side. Benson knelt and picked it up. "It's okay," he said, and touched a hand to her cheek. "He's just out there swimming, my dear." He swung his light toward the lake, to probe its black velvet stillness.

The light was swallowed up by darkness and distance. Somewhere far out across the water, a loon called its quavering lament.

"It's *not* okay," she said. "He can't swim. He wouldn't go out there. Not for fun."

"Then he's..." Benson didn't finish the thought. He turned over the shirt and smoothed a hand across its front. Quickly he drew something long and curved out of the breast pocket. "What the...?"

"You killed him," Meeka said matter-of-factly. Staring at Zundi's collar, she got to her feet. Eli had never liked fusses, and this had indeed become the mother of all fusses. He'd simply checked out, and Zundi had gone with him as she'd always gone.

"That's nonsense!" Benson said, rising also, then, when she turned away without answering, "Where do you think you're going?"

Away. She was simply fleeing the knife-sharp sorrow, but he caught her halfway up the trail.

"Meeka!" He pulled her around.

Choked by tears, she whirled, swinging as she turned. "It was you!" She hammered at his broad solid chest. "You killed him, you killed him, *you* killed him!"

"Easy! Take it easy." Benson folded her into a hug, pinning her arms to her sides, and drew her close. "Easy there."

"Y-you *killed* him!"

His chin brushed her hair as he shook his head. "No, I didn't, my dear."

"You did!" she sobbed. "You and the rest of them. Chasing him, hounding him, saying he'd go to jail. I told you Eli would never go to jail!"

"Meeka—" Benson's cheek rubbed the top of her head "—was he...? I mean, this is so senseless, so...was he crazy?"

Crazy in all the right ways. Remembering Eli's hundreds of whimsical kindnesses, she laughed a strangled little laugh that ended in tears. "No...he was just Eli."

For Meeka, numb with pain, the next hour passed in a blur. It was Benson who called the police from his car phone. Benson who discovered the folded issue of that day's paper on the seat of Eli's pickup with Eli's short message scribbled below the headline that accused him. "Sorry kid," it read, "but this ain't worth sticking around for. Zundi says to tell you *auf wiedersehen.* P.S. If you don't want Edward, put him in the duck pond. He'll do just fine." Benson who asked, "Who's Edward?"

"His goldfish—Edward, Prince of Tails," Meeka said between fresh sobs, and curled herself into a small, miserable ball in the front seat of the Jaguar.

So it was Benson who explained it all to Delbert Henley and Art Sugar, the night policeman, when they arrived at the lake. And finally it was Benson who drove her home to the farm.

He walked around to her side of the car, opened the door and put a hand on her shoulder. "Meeka?"

"You killed him." It was the first words she'd spoken in more than an hour.

"I think we'll talk about that tomorrow. Right now..." Gently he half lifted her out of the car. She swayed, and he looped an arm around her waist, holding her upright against him.

He'd killed Eli, and it felt heavenly to be held like this. That made no sense. She sucked in a ragged breath, inhaling the deeply male wonderfully comforting scent of him. Nothing made any sense at all tonight, but then, she'd been used to that state of affairs for some eight years now. Dreamily she let him turn her and direct her toward the house.

"Is there somebody I could call to come stay with you?" he asked as they reached the steps.

Beth, she thought. But then she'd have to explain, and she was too tired to explain. "No, I don't want anyone. *I want Eli.* Stop," she said when they'd trudged up to porch level. "I want to sit out here."

The nicotiana perfumed the velvety air, and the leaves whispered in the front-yard maples. Eli had always loved sitting out here in the dark.

"Sure." Benson settled her on the top step, then straightened. "I'll be right back."

She nodded indifferently, rested her head against a column and took another deep breath of the fragrant night. No hurry. She'd been doing nothing but hurrying these past few days. And now she couldn't imagine hurrying ever again. What was the use? Eli was—

"Here." Benson settled beside her. He caught her hand and set something cold between her fingers—a jelly jar. "This is wine, I take it?"

"Dandelion wine. Eli makes it every—" She stopped, let out a rusty little laugh, then drained the glass. Refrigerator cold, sweet and bitter, it blazed a trail of frigid fire down her throat. She gasped, then rested her head against the column. "Eli *made* it every spring," she said bitterly.

Benson put a glass to his lips and tried a sip. His shoulders jerked in a reflexive wince. "Here, I think you need this more than I do." He handed her the drink.

Without thinking, she downed that, as well, then set the glass aside.

For a while they sat there in silence. Benson eased himself down one step, then leaned back on his bent elbows. He tipped his head. "What smells so nice?" he asked, his voice very low.

"Nicotiana, petunias...some alyssum," she said, closing her eyes.

"You're the gardener?"

"Yes." Eli hadn't had the patience. "When I came here there weren't any flower beds. Seems like I plant a little more every year."

"When did you come here?" His voice was as gentle as a hand smoothing her hair.

"Eight years ago." She sighed and settled lower against the column. The night seemed warmer, or did the glow come from within—Eli's magical wine? Or... Dreamily she shook that thought aside. "My mother'd been dead about a year then and I'd been living with her cousin Mabel and her family, but they didn't want me." She shivered.

"Hard to believe," he murmured. "Eli was your mother's brother? Or your father's?"

She smiled. "He was no kin at all really, just a friend of my mother's."

"A friend?"

So he'd caught the note of ambiguity in her voice. He didn't miss much, did he? Her smile was bittersweet. "He loved her, I think. She'd lived here in town during her high-school years. I guess he met her then and fell for her, but she didn't feel that way about him. Then she met my father and left town with him."

"Who was your father?"

Funny how one big sorrow numbed all the little ones. Tonight she could have told this man anything. He was only a husky voice in the darkness, wrapping her in kindness as the lovely scents of her garden enfolded her. "A ski bum," she said. "Jamie Ranier. From out West somewhere. He'd come East to check out the skiing scene. He was a ski instructor up at Stowe. So that's where he took her... and where I was born."

Benson stirred, seemed nearer when he settled again. Eyes closed, she could feel his closeness through her skin. "And then?" he prompted.

"He stuck it out for almost three years. I can *just* remember him. His hair with the sun on it, him laughing as he lifted me over his head. And then he left. We don't get enough powder skiing in the East, you see. Too much ice."

Benson exhaled an angry breath. "He couldn't take you two with him?"

She shrugged. "Guess he didn't want to."

Warm, steady, his fingers curled around her ankle and simply held her. She let out a shaky breath. "Well, Mom had started her craft shop up in Stowe, and that was doing pretty well. She sold all kinds of wonderful yarns and knitting patterns. Maybe she didn't want to follow him." But even as she said it, she knew it wasn't so.

"And so when did Eli reappear?"

Meeka smiled. "I'm not sure. First time I remember him is at a picnic he took us on. It might have been my birthday. He pulled a tiny white mouse out of his pocket—it had a bow on its neck. That's the first thing I remember—his giving me Mousums." She smiled again. "After that, he'd just show up three or four times a year. He'd hang around the shop for a couple of days, talk to my mother, tease me, take us someplace strange or special, then he'd be gone again."

"Your mother never...?" Benson paused, his fingers brushing across her ankle as he searched for the words.

"Oh, I think she realized he loved her. You couldn't miss it. I even knew it, though I didn't think about it, any more than you think about air. He'd just sort of look at her. You know how a sunflower follows the sun all day? Like that."

"Poor bastard!" Benson muttered under his breath.

"I guess she couldn't help it. It wasn't that she was mean or that she didn't care," Meeka said, anxious for him to understand. "But I don't think she'd ever stopped loving my father, or hoping..."

His fingers tensed on her ankle. "Yes, I can see that."

"Maybe someday she'd have finally..." But Meeka didn't really think so. Though she'd never loved as her mother had loved, somehow she sensed the same terrible quality in herself. *To never be able to let go.* To love helplessly and forever, whether or not the one you loved was worthy.

She shivered and clasped her elbows hard. Perhaps this was why she'd hung back the few times she'd sensed a possibility. To give your heart to a stranger, then never be able to reclaim it—that was terrifying! Her mother had loved like that. Eli, also. Oh, love wasn't the sweet and gentle bringer of happiness the songs claimed it to be. Love latched on like a snapping turtle—latched on and held tight.

She shuddered again. "Anyway, whatever might have happened, instead, she died in a car wreck. Some damned drunk tourist ran her off the mountain one night." The memory lanced her shell of protective numbness like a white-hot needle—searing, sudden, as shocking as the first time. She reached for him, found his hand at her ankle and curled her fingers around his warm wrist. "So my cousin Mabel took me in, she and her husband."

Again he caught the undertones. "That was bad?"

"Yes." She didn't want to remember the loneliness, the hollow aching sadness of that year. She swallowed, then hurried through it. "I didn't... fit in. They had too many kids already—five of them—and I was different. I liked books, art, walking in the hills, going to school. They liked TV and, well, TV. They thought I was strange and snobby."

And Mabel's husband had wanted her to quit high school and care for the kids full-time so that Mabel could go back to work. She'd felt as if she were strangling, there in that tiny smelly house, with her future folding down upon her like a house of bright cards collapsing. "I was living out back of their place in an old travel trailer." She shivered. There'd been no electricity in the trailer, though she'd had her mother's down sleeping bag. But the blessed privacy had made the cold seem worthwhile.

Benson let her ankle go and shifted away.

Eyes closed, she sat very still, fighting the sense of loss, not sure if this was just an echo from the past, or...

His arm curled around her shoulders and he pulled her against him, settling her in the curve of his shoulder. "And then?" he murmured, his lips in her hair.

The peace rushed back, and a feeling of quiet spreading joy. Or perhaps this was a memory from the past, as well.

"Then Eli came. He asked me if I'd like to come live with him." She laughed deep in her throat, remembering how absurd the question had seemed. He'd needed to ask?

"And your cousin let you go—just like that?" An edge of anger hardened Benson's voice. "Let a kid go off with a strange man?"

"If you'd ever met Eli, that wouldn't shock you."

Benson snorted, and his arm firmed around her.

Funny, but even his anger made her feel good. She tipped her head back against his sheltering warmth and laughed under her breath. Now she was back into the good memories again. "Besides, he gave Mabel's husband his old VW van. We—Eli and Zundi and me—had to hitchhike back from Stowe in a snowstorm."

"He traded a van for you?" Benson repeated, incredulous.

She nodded happily. "Guess they wanted something for all the trouble I'd given them. I guess I was a pretty stubborn, mouthy kid."

"Still..."

She shrugged and felt her nerves tremble and stir at the feel of her arm sliding against his chest. "It worked, didn't it? Everyone got what they wanted."

"But the authorities... nobody objected?" Benson still sounded outraged.

"He made it official—got all the papers he needed somehow, claiming custody and allowing me to go to school here."

Then it hit her, and Meeka sat upright. Eli hadn't had those papers at first, had he, since he'd kept her out of school and tutored her for the rest of that winter. And yet suddenly, by summer, he'd had all the necessary documents! She laughed aloud. Cousin Mabel hadn't given him the papers, she'd bet, now that she thought of it. She laughed again, turning to smile up at Benson. Eli had forged the necessary papers—she'd bet her bottom dollar!

Her laughter caught in her throat at the look on Benson's face. *Here I'm laughing about forgery, when—*

Dipping his head, he kissed her.

At the touch of his lips, she gasped, and the kiss deepened. He tasted as dark and fragrant as the night. His beard rasped her cheek. Then it was over as suddenly as it had begun.

"Well, it may not bother *you,*" he said roughly. Abruptly he pulled away.

Bothered her, it didn't *bother* her exactly. It felt as if the night had done one slow somersault—with her inside it. Meeka sucked in a slow experimental breath. Sat staring up at him.

Benson stood abruptly. "Traded you for a van," he marveled. "This whole place is crazy! I'm in another world—or maybe out of it." He touched her hair, then backed away a step. "And George Washington's a traitor, not a hero." He laughed under his breath. "'The whole world turned upside down...' Maybe I'm still climbing mountains in Bolivia and this is all a dream. Or I fell on my head."

Funny, that was how she felt—exactly.

He knelt before her, lifted her hands and kissed them. "Will you be all right if I leave you now? I don't think I should..." His voice trailed away.

Eli and Zundi were dead, and she felt as if the sun were rising inside her. Meeka shook her head at the wonder of it all.

"You won't be? Then—"

She shook her head violently. "No, I didn't mean that! I'll be fine." With him still holding her hands, she stood. Suddenly she needed to get away. She *couldn't* be feeling what she was feeling. "You'd better go!"

"Yes," he agreed, not releasing her.

"And I'll go to bed," she added, taking a step back.

Her foot kicked the jelly jar, and it rolled across the boards with a chuckling sound. That explained it! This was all Eli's fault—his potent, magical dandelion wine. It had gone to her head. "I'll go to bed," she repeated. But she knew she wouldn't sleep. She wanted to dance, she wanted to— She shook her head and backed away another step.

"Good," he said, and released her. "I think that's a good idea, and I'll go—" he glanced over his shoulder, as if suddenly realizing where he was "—somewhere," he finished lamely. But he still stood there, staring after her as she backed through her front door and closed it between them.

He didn't move from her porch until she'd fallen fully clothed on her bed. Hugging herself hard, staring up at the blackness of her ceiling, Meeka at last heard his soft footsteps. Slowly they descended the front steps, then paused again on the gravel of the walk as if he'd stopped to stare up at her windows.

A minute later she heard the grumble of his car's engine, which receded into the distance as he backed down the drive. Headlights swept across her ceiling, then darkness flowed back again.

CHAPTER SEVEN

SHE WAS SWIMMING in the lake. Water slid across her naked limbs in a silken caress. She ducked underwater, then surfaced, gasping with pleasure. As she shook silver drops out of her eyes, a birchbark canoe glided past—so close she could see the black pattern of a knot in its side, like one eye winking. In its stern, Benson steered with merciless precision. In the bow, Eli paddled for dear life. Their gazes intent on some far horizon, neither man spared her a glance.

"Wait!" she cried. But her mouth dipped underwater, and the sound came out in choking bubbles. *Oh, wait!*

Perched in the bow of the canoe, Zundi looked back and opened her mouth. "Bing bong!" she barked.

Heart pounding, still gasping for breath, Meeka rolled over and sat up.

Bing bong!

"Whooh!" Hand to her forehead, she started to laugh. A dream. Only a dream. Then she remembered. Eli. "Oh, God!"

Boooonng!

"Who the...?" Pushing the covers aside, she went to the window.

Three men and two women stood on the front walk staring up at her. "She's awake!" cried one of the women to someone up on the porch, who was mashing her doorbell.

"Ms. Ranier!" called the tallest man, looking sympathetic and avid all at once. "I'm Peterson of the *New York Times*. Would you care to make a statement about the tragic death of your uncle, Eli Trou— Hey!" he yelped as Meeka's favorite vase smashed at his feet. "I'm from the *Times!*"

"And I'm making a statement!" Meeka yelled, looking for something else to throw. Grabbing her wastebasket, she aimed for the reporter in the flowered hat, who fled, squeaking, for the shelter of the nearest maple. "You killed my uncle! All of you. How's that for a statement?"

But there was no one left on the lawn to take notes. From beneath the porch roof, she could hear a muttered conference going on.

"Well, of course she's upset."

"Not as upset as my editor will be if I don't get him something I can use. Why can't they find the damned body?"

"You try her, Emily. You've got a trustworthy face."

"Vultures!" Meeka hollered, then headed for the bathroom. They'd killed Eli just as surely as if they'd held a gun to his head and pulled the trigger, she thought as she turned on the shower and stepped into the stall. They and Cameron Benson. Ducking her head beneath the spray, she let the delicious warmth sluice over her—and remembered the hard, hot feel of his mouth on hers. She shuddered and crossed her arms over her breasts. Had she really let him kiss her? And reveled in that kissing? Eli's killer? How could she?

Seizing her washcloth, she scrubbed furiously at her lips. But the memory didn't wash away. It lasted through two latherings with her favorite shampoo, right through the cream rinse, then followed her back to the bedroom. Swearing, she threw her towel across the bed. How could she be thinking of him when—

"Meeeeka!" a familiar voice called through the window in a furious undertone. "Where the heck are you?"

"Beth?" Meeka caught the towel to her chest and ran to the window.

Below on the front walk, Beth Higgins peered toward the road, then whirled and gave a start. "Oh, there you are! Get down here quick as you can! He can't hold them for long."

"Who can't hold who?"

"Your friend Benson. He's giving the reporters an interview out on the road. So move it! Meet me in three minutes at the barn—and you've still got clothes at my place, so for heaven's sake don't stop to pack!"

When Meeka joined her minutes later, Beth dragged her toward the woods. "I'm parked over on Tilden's back lane. And I brought a blanket along. You can lie down and we'll throw that over you till we get to town."

"But how did you hook up with Benson?" Meeka panted.

"He brought my car back this morning. Said he'd asked at the Coffee Pot who was your best friend in town, and Betsy told him me, so he guessed it was mine. Then he told me the news about Eli, and Meeka, I'm so sorry!" Beth slowed as they reached the cover of the woods. "I'm *so* sorry, Meek," she repeated, and turning, gave her friend a hug.

"Yeah, me, too," Meeka mumbled against Beth's shoulder, her eyes blurring. "Can't believe it yet, really."

"I know." Beth patted her back. "I know. Anyway, Benson said the press would be driving you crazy for a statement, so we worked up a diversion. Guess they're driving him crazy, instead."

Serves him right, Meeka thought to herself.

And she hadn't changed her mind later in the day when Benson stopped by the Higgins's house. "Tell him I don't want to see him," she told Beth. "Now or ever."

"He's been out to the lake," Beth said, frowning her disapproval.

"If he's got any news, he can tell it to you."

She didn't dare see him. During this endless day of waiting, her sorrow had deepened and widened into an emotion she didn't dare name. People had been leaving her all her life, but she'd never thought that Eli would let her down. What good would it do now to blame Eli, who was past hearing, who couldn't even be found to be blamed?

That left only Cameron Benson as a focus for this child-like, aching, incredulous rage. She wanted to stamp her feet, beat on his solid chest, cry *no* and *no* and *no* till he— "No." Swallowing around the lump in her throat, she shook her head. "No, I can't—I won't—see him. If they find... anything, Ric will come tell me." One of the town's volunteer firemen, Beth's husband was helping to drag the lake.

"Still haven't found a thing," Ric reported wearily when he stopped by the house for supper a few hours later. "But that's not surprising."

It wasn't. The lake had been their childhood swimming hole. As kids, they'd taken a gruesome, shivery delight in tales that it was bottomless. Growing up, they'd lost their belief in such tales. Still, the lake was extremely deep, its bottom pocked with crevices and boulders.

"If we don't find him this evening, Art Sugar says we'll just have to wait till he... ouch!" Ric gave Beth a wounded look across the table.

"Do I hear somebody at the front door?" Beth caroled, looking in that direction. She blinked when a knock sounded faintly. "Why, it is! I mean, er... Ric, would you answer that?"

"If it's Cameron Benson, I won't see him," Meeka declared. Avoiding Beth's eyes, she sighed and set her fork down.

Ric returned with a puzzled frown and a large manila envelope. "For you, I guess," he said, handing it to Meeka. "From a fellow I never saw before. Said somebody over in Bennington paid him fifty dollars to deliver it."

The address on the front of the envelope was typed. "'M.R.,'" Meeka read aloud, "'care of Beth Higgins, 27 Bailey Avenue.'"

Her eyes moved to a line at the bottom right corner. "Open in private," it said. She frowned. No one knew she was hiding here except Cameron Benson. But why would Benson send her something from Bennington? Or send it via a stranger?

Her heart knocked against her ribs and kept on knocking as she stood up from the table. "Would you excuse me?"

In the guest bedroom, she sat on the bed. Fingers trembling, she tore open the flap, then drew out a large photograph.

Colored in the golds and sepias of an antique daguerreotype, the photo's two subjects swam before her widening eyes. She let out a wordless whimper of disbelief.

This was one of those staged photos, where tourists dress up in historical costume and pose for the camera. The setting was a Western saloon.

Seated stiffly in a wooden chair, a bottle of whiskey and a pack of cards on the table beside him, Eli sported a ten-gallon hat. He'd pulled the brim down at a rakish angle—only his luxuriant mustache and a broad grin showed below it. He wore a moth-eaten, woolly vest. His skinny legs were clad in a pair of buckskin chaps. And he held a six-shooter braced nonchalantly across one knee.

On the floor beside him, Zundi sat upright on her fat haunches. The battered brown fedora she wore covered all of her face but her black shiny nose and her white crocodile teeth. A feather boa was looped twice around her stubby neck, then slung jauntily to one side. Hands down, she made the shortest ugliest Woman of Easy Virtue that the West had ever seen. Undaunted, she flapped her paws at the camera, no doubt begging for a tidbit held by the unseen photographer.

"Oh, Eli!" Laughing through her tears, Meeka turned the photo over and saw the inscription in Eli's familiar hand:

> Reports of my death have been somewhat exaggerated, but please don't tell a soul. (Except for Beth.)

"Eli, I will never, never, *never* forgive you!" Meeka swore. She fell backward on the bed and held the message overhead.

> P.S. You didn't really dump Edward in the pond, did you? I'm sure he'd do fine, but he's used to the soft life.
> P.S.S. Catch you before the snow flies, kid, if not sooner.

"Before the snow flies," Meeka muttered the next morning as she parked her car on a side street near the bank. But early as winters came in Vermont, Eli was still talking months.

That wouldn't do, she thought grimly as she twisted her hair into a knot at the nape of her neck and clipped it. Look how much havoc Eli had raised in three short days—a protest parade, getting the town to drag the lake for him. Give him three months on the loose and he might bring the whole country tumbling down around their ears! Why, only that morning the television news had featured an interview with the vice president, who'd gamely insisted that George Washington was a true-blue American patriot.

But he'd been followed by a historian, a psychiatrist and a document expert who'd maintained that all along they'd thought George looked pretty darned sneaky when you looked closely at his portraits. They didn't doubt for a minute that the letter would prove to be authentic.

At that Meeka had switched channels, only to find herself staring at Cameron Benson, with a dozen microphones waving in his face. It had taken her a moment to realize that this was the interview to which he'd submitted as she'd made her escape the day before. Looking as if he'd dearly love to feed the mike to the reporter holding it, Benson had simply explained, then explained again, then repeated once more through clenched teeth, that he had no intention of releasing the letter until his panel of experts finished their analysis and reached their verdict.

"And is it true that you'd threatened to sue the late Eli Trout for fraud, for his part in selling you the letter, Mr. Benson?"

A muscle had jumped in Benson's lean cheek. "That's not true. Not exactly."

"And if you accused the late Mr. Trout of fraud, then presumably you think the George Washington letter is a fake! Could you tell the American people why, in that case, your magazine would choose to publish—"

Even on camera, Meeka had been able to see the blood rising in the publisher's face. "End of interview, people," he'd interrupted coolly, "and I believe you'll find that, in the meantime, Ms. Ranier has flown the—"

The camera had cut to a network anchor. Her perky face belying her somber lines, she'd chirped something about the anguish of a nation whose trust in its most cherished hero was tottering— Meeka had switched the set off. Her own feelings had been muddled by the sight of Benson holding the pack at bay on her behalf. Guilt and gratitude and admiration and resentment still roiled wildly in her stomach.

Meeka settled Beth's flowered straw hat on her head, added a pair of sunglasses with screaming red horn-rim frames that she'd also borrowed from her friend, then studied the effect in the car mirror. People who knew her would wonder what kind of fit she'd taken. But it should do to deceive the reporters, most of whom had never more than glimpsed her. Sliding out of the station wagon, she glanced back as she passed its rear window.

She'd folded down the rear seat, then jammed the mattress from the guest room at the farm into the space created. Her sleeping bag was tossed in on top of the mattress, as was the small cook stove she favored on camping trips, her hiking boots, a tent, a topographic map of the Green Mountains and other assorted gear.

She hoped she wouldn't be needing all that, but if she did, she was ready. The one thing Meeka did know was that she wasn't coming back to town without Eli. Which was what brought her to the bank. If she was going Eli-hunting, she'd need money for food and gas.

Taking her place in line for a teller, Meeka surveyed the room from beneath her hat brim. Bob Cadwaller was just counting his cash at the counter. He turned, still counting, and walked right past her.

Good. Old Mrs. Biddle was next in line, but everyone knew she couldn't see past the end of her beaky nose. And there wasn't a reporter in the place. With a smile of relief, Meeka turned toward the front door. Her smile froze.

Swaggering as if heading a military drum corps, Justin Hawthorne marched into the bank. When his gaze fell on Meeka, his usual self-important scowl deepened. "Have they found him yet?" he boomed, advancing on her.

So much for disguises! "N-no. No, they haven't." Hugging her elbows, she turned her back on him and faced the counter.

"Well, Eli got what he deserved!" rumbled Hawthorne.

Meeka couldn't believe her ears. Turning around, she tipped her hat back to a fighting angle and brought her glasses to the tip of her nose. Eli was alive, of course, but Hawthorne didn't know that. "I beg your pardon?"

"In fact, drowning was too good for him," the innkeeper forged on. "We used to take traitors out and shoot 'em."

Meeka whipped off her glasses and tapped him on his barrel chest with an earpiece. "You *personally* shot traitors?" she inquired, her voice quivering with contempt.

"I, er, would have, if I'd been there," Hawthorne amended.

"How sad that you missed all the fun," Meeka said sweetly. "Maybe you should have tried the Vietnam War if you really wanted to shoot people. Or was that one too close for comfort?"

Hawthorne's florid face turned a satisfying shade of strawberry. "I'll have you know that I volunteered for the marines, but because of my flat feet..." With strawberry deepening to brick, he made a broad motion of dismissal. "But that's not what we're talking about. We're talking about a forging, libeling traitor who got what was coming to him. Good riddance!"

"Oh, there you are," observed a smooth, masculine voice. Stepping around Hawthorne, Cameron Benson dropped an arm around Meeka's shoulders. He turned to look Hawthorne up and down. "Don't believe I know you," he said, his voice dangerously polite.

Though Hawthorne had served in no real war, he knew when the tactical odds had changed. He retreated a step and bristled. "Nor I you," he responded, giving the younger man a curt nod. "But if you're a friend of Ms. Ranier, then you're no friend of George Washington—nor of any real American. Good day." With another contemptuous nod, he did a parade-ground pivot and marched out of the bank.

"Who the devil was that?" Benson asked, looking after him.

"Number one flag waver in Buxton," Meeka said absently. But she wasn't thinking about Hawthorne—wasn't really thinking at all. It was what she was feeling, this strange sense of...of rightness. She shivered suddenly. Whatever it was, it was as frightening as it was seductive.

His arm tightened slightly, which brought her shoulder to rest against his heart. "And you?" he asked softly. "How have you been?"

Meeka swallowed and saw his eyes flick to that tiny convulsion. "Oh... okay." She turned out from under his arm and glanced toward the teller.

Hilda May sat with her chin propped on her clasped hands, watching them with open fascination.

"Hiya, Hilda May." Careful to keep her back between Benson and the counter, Meeka whipped out the check she'd already made out and handed it to the teller. "Could I cash that, please?"

But her discretion was wasted. "Two hundred dollars!" squawked Hilda May. "This'll just about close you out, Meeka."

"Yep," Meeka agreed, gritting her teeth. When she'd received her money and Hilda May's condolences about Eli, she turned from the window. "Good to see you," she said as she sailed past Benson.

But his steps sounded on the floor behind her, then his hand swept up to open the door. "You're in a hurry," he noted as he fell into step.

"Yes." And how was she to get rid of him? She had no intention of telling him or anyone that Eli was alive till she'd gotten her hands on the rascal and delivered him to Mr. Finley.

"So when can we talk?"

"Talk?" Perching her garish sunglasses back on her nose, she surveyed the street. Should she proceed to her car? Or try to lose him? But this wasn't New York City, where presumably you could dash in the front door of Sak's, lose your tail in the lingerie department, then duck out a side door. She supposed she could take him to the Coffee Pot, then try to escape through the kitchen. But it wouldn't be exactly subtle.

"Yes, talk." Benson caught her arm and swung her to face him. "I still have to account for that letter to some two hundred and fifty million people, Meeka." Gently he lifted her glasses off her nose. "I don't want to intrude on your grief, but we've got to discuss..." His eyes sharpened. Then, slowly, one dark brow raked upward. He glanced down at her glasses, then up at her face.

"What?" she asked defensively, taking them back.

"Interesting mourning clothes, I was thinking." As the guilty flush crept up her cheeks, his grip tightened. The publisher frowned. "You don't..." He drew a fingertip across her lips.

She couldn't help it. She smiled, then looked away.

"Meeka?" Benson hooked a finger against her chin and brought her gaze back to his. His golden eyes unwavering as a cat's at a mousehole, he studied her. "You don't look sad. What gives?"

"Nothing!" She glanced away again. Her face was so pink now her eyes were watering. "Oh," she said suddenly as her gaze focused on the group leaving the Coffee Pot. Reporters. And they'd spotted her, too. One pointed, then they all wheeled in her direction. "Uh-oh!"

"Miss Ranier!" one of them yelled. "Wait! Just a question!"

As she broke into a run, Meeka scrounged in her pocket for her keys. Beside her, Benson was keeping pace. "Take me along," he demanded as they reached her car.

"I can't." Absurdly she wished she could.

As she started the engine, he bent down to peer in the window behind her. "Camping gear? Where are you going?"

"Wait! Please wait!" yelled a reporter. He was closing the gap fast.

"Away," she said hurriedly. "I need to... to forget."

"Eli's not dead, is he?" Benson leaned down to stare into her face. "That's why you're smiling. You're taking supplies to him, or—"

"Watch your toes," Meeka cautioned as she pulled out from the curb. Swearing, Benson fell back just as the first reporter reached her car.

"Wait!" he yelled, and slapped her back window in frustration.

Instead, Meeka stomped on the gas pedal.

But if she could leave the press in her dust, Cameron Benson was another matter. Half an hour north of Buxton, Meeka checked her rearview and there he was, his black Jaguar filling the mirror. His headlights flashed three times—no doubt a command to pull over.

"That's what you think!" she growled, keeping her foot to the floor. Now what? There was no way to outrun him. No way to lose him, when her way was enclosed by mountains to the left and right. "I'll think of something," she swore, shaking her head stubbornly when his horn sounded behind her.

But in the end, it was more luck than planning that helped Meeka escape. As they swept into Bennington, the town from which Eli's envelope had been sent, Benson still dogged her back bumper. At an intersection ahead, the light was green. Meeka slowed. If she could run that light at the last possible moment... Eyes on the traffic signal, she didn't notice the elderly woman with a cane who'd stepped out from the curb. "Oh!" she cried as she saw her. She swerved to the left, missing the woman by a wide margin. "Sorry!" she gasped, looking back.

Standing in the street, the old lady scowled after her. "Sorry," Meeka muttered again and sped up. The light switched to yellow.

As she swept under the changing light, Meeka looked back. The old lady was venting her wrath on Benson. Commanding the middle of the lane, she shook her cane at his windshield. His Jaguar crouched like a scolded cat, with more traffic stacking up behind him. As Meeka hooked a swift right onto a side road, she saw her blue-haired savior saunter across the street, chin regally high and cane rapping the pavement in brisk triumph. Giggling, Meeka turned right again, doubling back.

After hiding her car in the depths of a repair garage—at the cost of an oil change—she spent the rest of the day tracking down Bennington's few photography shops.

Since Eli's photo had been sent from Bennington, Meeka assumed it had been taken here. It made sense, after all. Bennington was a brisk bike ride from the lake. And that was how Eli had made his getaway—she'd figured that out once she knew he was alive.

Eli's mountain bike was missing from their locked barn. Apparently he'd stopped by the farm sometime during the day of his "suicide," after Ric and Beth had lured the reporters away and Meeka had fled into town. He'd put the bike in his pickup and driven to the lake.

After he'd set up his "drowning," he'd pedaled off into the night, no doubt with his saddlebags stuffed with camping gear and Zundi riding as she always did behind his seat in the attached plastic crate.

The clerk at the first camera store had no idea where such a photo could have been taken. He sent her to another shop, where Meeka found a note on the door stating that the proprietor was photographing a wedding and would be back "shortly."

"Shortly," of course, was a relative term. She spent the afternoon cooling her heels at the soda fountain of the drugstore across the street. She'd just concluded that she'd wasted her day when a glance through the window showed her a camera-laden man unlocking the shop door.

"Wasn't taken in this town," the proprietor said firmly when she showed him Eli's photo. "But a girl came in with one of these yesterday wanting a frame for it—a shot of herself dressed up like a floozy and her boyfriend as a gambler. Makes you wonder how folks see 'emselves."

"Where was hers taken?" Meeka asked, and held her breath.

"Hmm," the proprietor said, apparently dragging the answer out from someplace deep inside. "There's a fair going on, out Route 100. Jaycees, or some such, run it every summer. Believe she got it there."

A fair! Now that was exactly the sort of thing to attract Eli.

But the question was, would anybody at the fair remember him? Looking down at the photo as she returned it to her bag, Meeka smiled. Of course they would. How could they not?

CHAPTER EIGHT

BACK AT THE GARAGE, the mechanic had drained her car of oil, then stopped that job to do a rush repair for a loyal customer. Two frustrating hours passed before he returned to the task.

Still, there had been one good thing about her delay, Meeka thought, when at last she headed out of town. By now, Benson was sure to have given up his search and moved on. With that satisfying thought, she rounded a bend and found herself gaping at the Jaguar, parked next to the pumps at a service station. She didn't spot Benson in the moment before her reflexes took over and she stomped on the gas pedal. With luck he hadn't seen her.

But his car was pointed in the same direction, she reminded herself, pressing harder on the pedal. Her ancient station wagon emitted an abused groan and a blat of smoke, then gradually responded. Swearing, Meeka checked the rearview mirror. There were four cars behind her. But if one of them was Benson, it was now too dark to see.

So be it. She didn't look back again, for what was the use? Instead, she devoted her attention to road signs, and at last she saw what she'd been looking for.

"Jaycees' Summer Fair" proclaimed a banner arching across a side road. Meeka turned left, then winced as the third set of headlights behind her turned, as well. Turning again, she rattled across a field filled with parked cars.

Up ahead, a row of bleachers rose against the darkening sky. Beyond them, red, green and gold lights revolved and glittered. A midway ride shaped like a giant, light-spangled hammer reared with ominous deliberation above the bleachers, then vanished in a whirling arc.

Meeka cut her engine and heard the distant shrieks of terror and delight. In spite of her worry, she smiled. Eli's kind of place.

Picking her way through the rows of cars, she glanced several times over her shoulder. But if Benson was in pursuit, she didn't see him. And even if he was, there was quite a crowd in which to lose herself.

Scruffy teenagers strolled with arms around each other's waists, sharing cotton candy and sticky kisses. Clutching gigantic pink pandas or goofy stuffed giraffes, children darted and swooped. Families with toddlers trudged purposefully toward the mounting din of screams and pounding rock music. Other families straggled back to their cars. A small boy let go of his helium balloon, then wailed as it rose toward the stars.

Parked nearest the ticket booth, a long row of gleaming motorcycles had attracted its own admiring crowd. Sporting a uniform of tattered black T-shirts, tight black jeans, greasy ponytails and lewd tattoos, two muscle-bound bikers stood guard. One lounged against a bike and cleaned his nails with a buck knife. The other chewed tobacco, spit and leered at the passing women.

Meeka paid her admission, then passed under another banner and out onto the football field. She stopped and laughed aloud. The midway rides swooped, spun, rose and fell. Each ride was encrusted with lights, making the night pulse and twinkle with shades of green, ruby, silver and gold. A ride like an enormous jewel box whirled to a pulsing rock beat. The next, called the Tomahawk, rose to form a gigantic golden X against the velvet sky, then slashed down while its riders shrieked.

Meeka started down a row of sideshow booths and coin-toss games. Stalking back and forth before a gaudy facade billed as the Ring of Fire, a barker cajoled the passing crowd with his gravelly singsong: "See the Riiing of Fire. Join your friends and neighbors, folks! It's a thrill a minute! A *spill* a minute! Thundering, *death*-defying motorcycles in a riiing of fire! Huuurry on *down* if you intend to go! Next show starts in fiiive minutes! Bring your *girl*friend, bring somebody *else's* girlfriend. Hurry on *down!* What about you, little lady? You look like you could use a thrill."

Meeka smiled, shook her head and walked on. She glanced back to see half a dozen bikers muscle their way to the head of the waiting line, then stand there, bulging, tattooed arms folded, in grim anticipation.

Her eyes drifted past them, then widened. Cameron Benson stood just inside the entrance gates, his eyes scanning the field.

Blast! Meeka whirled, then ducked around a knock-over-the-bottle booth. She couldn't shake the man—she was a human magnet, and he the steel! From the far side of the booth she peeped through a forest of dangling stuffed animals. But Benson had vanished.

"How about you, sweetheart? Three throws for a quarter. A prize every time," declared a carny, offering three wooden hoops.

"No, thanks," Meeka said, but doubted if he could hear her. The overamplified songs of the midway rides blended into one throbbing cacophony. She cut through a queue of people snaking back from a hot-dog stand, then stopped short.

Before a blue-and-white-striped tent, an easel displayed dozens of "antique" photographs. Meeka studied the samples, then smiled. From the middle of the board, two familiar desperadoes grinned back at her.

"Only twelve dollars," said the woman seated at a card table by the easel. "Or tell you what, honey—for you a bargain. Ten for a single girl."

"Actually, I was wondering when you took this one." Meeka pointed.

The woman's thin lips tightened. "Why'd you want to know?"

"That's my uncle—Eli."

Her plucked eyebrows rose in a skeptical shrug. "Night before last."

"You didn't happen to talk to him, did you? He didn't say where he was going?" Meeka asked eagerly.

"If he wanted you to know, I guess he'd have told you himself, wouldn't he?"

"Please!" Meeka clutched at the edge of the table. "Eli's in trouble. I'm only trying to help him."

"Who's in trouble?" demanded a burly man, stepping out of the tent. This, apparently, was the photographer.

"My uncle." Meeka pulled out her copy of Eli's photo. "He sent me this."

The photographer scowled. "I knew that ol' geezer was nothin' but trouble. I told Gabriella not to take him on."

"Shut up, Harry!" the woman snapped. She glared at Meeka. "Listen, we're minding our own business and trying to make a living. Now, do you want a photo, or do you want to shove off?"

"Take him on—you mean he's here?" Meeka gasped. But of course he was! What better place to hide than a carnival? Eli must have felt he'd died and gone to heaven. "Where is he?" She looked around wildly and her eyes alighted on a familiar hawk-nosed profile. Three booths back, Benson stood talking to a man in uniform—a policeman.

"Oops!" Meeka took to her heels, dodged around a tent serving fried doughnuts and cider, ducked past a man who guessed people's weights and ages, then found herself standing in a lane lined with mechanical rides.

At the end of the row, aglow like a fairy-tale chrysanthemum with lights of red, gold, orange and turquoise, a gigantic wheel turned above everything else—the tallest ferris wheel she'd ever seen. From up there she'd have a bird's-eye view of the fairgrounds, as well as a hiding place.

It didn't hit her till she stood in line that she hadn't purchased a ticket for the ride. Meeka dug into her pocket and pulled out a five-dollar bill.

The man ushered a couple into their chair, and they spun up into the night. He turned, then scowled at Meeka's bill. "Gotta have a ticket, honey."

"I forgot to buy one. You couldn't just..."

The man started to shake his head, then paused as a hand reached past Meeka, holding a twenty.

"You'd be doing us a favor," Benson said, taking Meeka's arm.

"Well, if you put it like that..." The twenty vanished into the operator's shirt pocket. "Step this way."

"Um, I don't think..." Meeka stammered as Benson steered her to the chair. "I mean, thanks, but—"

"My pleasure." Benson's smile was ironic as he sat, then pulled her down beside him. The restraining bar snapped into place. Their seat jerked, then rocked free as the ferris wheel rolled.

Wind like cool silk lifted her hair as the lights fell away below. "Very smooth," Meeka admitted. She tried to frown, but her face muscles couldn't pull it off. Instead, she smiled. This was lovely—crazy, but lovely.

Benson didn't return her smile, but his dark eyes danced. Or perhaps it was only the reflection of the lights of the carnival. The wheel stopped to take on more passengers, and they hung, suspended halfway up the arc. "How could I resist?" he said, draping his arm around her shoulders.

Unable to sustain his teasing gaze, Meeka looked away, staring out at the glitter and whirl. The wheel turned again and they lifted with a rush, the raucous music falling away, the chair reaching for the serenity of a midnight-blue sky. This time they stopped at the very top of the arc. The fairgrounds spread out below in a crazy quilt of movement and color.

"Besides," Benson continued, "you're hard to corner."

And now he had her well and truly cornered! The wheel turned again, and this time the ride started. They swept toward the ground at a dizzying pace. The music swelled, the odors of popcorn and charcoal grills rose to meet them. "Eli's alive, isn't he?" Benson said.

Tell no one, Eli had written. But she couldn't lie, not to this man. Trapped, Meeka looked at him steadily. Cast by the wheel's supporting struts, shadows rippled and fled across his angular face. He had a wonderful mouth, strong, beautifully shaped, with an odd sensitive quirk to the corners. And she knew already how it felt on hers.

"And you're in on this," Benson continued, his face hardening when she still didn't speak. He twisted to grasp the seat behind her, bracketing her with his arms. "It's been a swindle from day one, hasn't it? A faked letter, a faked death when the going got rough? But how you can look like that and be in on this—" He shook his head angrily. "And knowing that you are, how I can still want to kiss you..." His laughter was bitter, self-mocking. "It makes no sense. *I've* got more sense than that."

"You always have to be sensible?" But Meeka knew as she asked that it must be so. Clearly he came from an orderly, rational world, where he was the actor, not the acted upon. He shaped life to suit him. To be out of control, to float through the world not knowing where he'd land or how—as she'd lived much of her life—yes, that would be outside his realm.

Slowly he shook his head. His mouth was coming closer. His fingers brushed her neck, then entwined themselves in her hair. As his mouth came down on hers, they reached the top of their orbit, then sank in a dizzying rush.

He seemed to sink into her. As she closed her eyes, her arms rose to pull him closer. Pounding music surged up to envelop them. The blood pounded her own heart's echo into her ears. She whimpered against his lips and tried to squirm closer. His arms tightened around her ribs till she gasped, and their breaths mingled.

The wheel glided to a stop and they hung, rocking. At last, Benson lifted his head. "That irrational enough for you?" He brought his hands to her shoulders, then pushed himself away in a slow, painful movement. "It's too damned crazy for me!" With a fingertip that shook ever so slightly, he drew a line from her eyebrows, down her nose, then traced the curve of her lips. "Though it makes its own kind of crazy sense, I suppose. You're very beautiful. Too damned beautiful to be true."

Odd that he should think so. No one else had ever seen that in her. And yet, wonderful as that was, it wasn't enough. He thought she was a crook. She and Eli.

His fingertip traced her lips again. She caught his wrist and pulled his hand aside. "If that's what you think..." Then she shouldn't—couldn't—let him touch her like this. There could be no respect, no real caring, if he thought her a swindler. He simply liked kissing her, as any man liked kissing. She'd be a fool to take it for more than that.

He didn't try to kiss her again. The chair moved, lifting them to the top of its arc, then stopping once more as passengers were unloaded. To the west, a range of black mountains kindled to purple with inner fire, then went dark again—a line of thunderheads, not mountains at all.

Benson slouched back in the seat, his shoulder warm against hers. He let out a hiss between his teeth and glared up at the stars. "So where's your uncle?" he said flatly. "Here?"

Meeka shrugged. At the moment she hardly cared. Her eyes surveyed the fairground. So many people down there, all of them with their own heartbreaks and hidden desires—then her eyes stopped. Far off, a red sausage-shaped dog trotted across an open stretch of the field—Zundi, or another dachshund equally rotund. Holding a bouquet of pink cotton candy, a small boy chased after her.

The dachshund turned, then stood at bay as the child approached, hand outstretched. So it wasn't Zundi, Meeka concluded. Zundi had never liked children, though she was just the size to fascinate them. The boy leaned closer. The dog submitted to a timid pat, then lunged, turned and waddled away—a large swath of pink trailing over its shoulder as it fled with a mouthful of cotton candy. Meeka laughed. Oh, that was Zundi, all right!

"What's so funny?" Benson asked as their chair reached the platform.

"Nothing. Everything." Meeka put her own troubles out of mind. It was Eli she should be worrying about. But first she had to shake Benson. They started down the platform stairs, the publisher holding her arm in a casual grip. But she knew better than to try to break it.

"Like some gum?" She pulled a pack from her pocket, along with the bill she'd deposited there. With a flick of the fingers, she sent that sailing over the side of the staircase. She made a grab for it and missed. "Darn! My five!"

It fluttered down to the litter-strewn ground behind the platform. "I'll get it." Benson swung over the railing, then dropped. "Do you see it?"

"Behind you," Meeka called. When he turned, she plunged down the last few stairs and headed in the direction that Zundi had fled. A double row of tents edged the far side of the center field. Panting, she turned to look over her shoulder, but saw no sign of Benson. Desperately, she scanned the lane. *Eli, where in blue blazes are you?*

The fourth tent down on the opposite side was topped by red, fluttering pennants and a gaudy banner, on which crescent moons and stars glittered against a background of purple. Golden letters announced Madame Gabriella Knows All! A smaller sign hung from the tent eaves offering Fortunes and Advice—$5.

Gabriella. Yes—that was the name!

A line of three women waited before the lantern-lit tent. They shifted restlessly and their movement revealed two larger-than-life silhouettes cast onto the canvas wall by the light within.

Across a table, the shadow of a woman faced the shadow of a man. And there was no mistaking the man's angular profile. Eli had always looked like a white-haired version of Ichabod Crane or an underfed Lincoln.

With a laugh, Meeka started around the women. "Excuse me, but—"

"But nothing!" exclaimed the first one in line, a redhead wearing a skimpy red tube top. She lifted a skinny arm to block Meeka's way. "Wait your turn."

"But that's a...friend of mine in there, and I need to—"

"You need to mind your manners, honey, or we'll mind them for you," drawled the second woman. She was dressed in skintight denim, studded with silver rivets. A small rose tattoo formed a beauty mark at the edge of her lips.

Biker women, Meeka realized, taking a step back. "Sorry! I can wait." She'd have to if she didn't want her teeth shoved down her throat. She stole a glance over her shoulder, saw no sign of Benson, then took her place at the end of the line. As she turned to watch Eli's gesturing shadow, she noticed another sign pinned by the entrance to the tent: How Well Do You Know Your Lover? Your Boss? Your Self? Handwriting Reveals All! Analysis By Eli The Perspicacious—$5."

Inside, the shadow of the woman stood, then grew gigantic as she approached. A bleached blonde dressed in a black leather jumpsuit pushed through the tent flaps. "Phew!" she said to the redhead, "He told me things about me my own momma doesn't know!"

"Yeah?" her friend replied. "Let's see what he makes of this!" She pulled a folded paper from her hip pocket and marched into the tent.

Meeka sighed. She'd hoped that Eli would come to the door to welcome his next customer.

"What was that?" the bleached blonde wondered.

"Poem Manny wrote her," replied one of her companions. "But what'd the guy say about you?"

"Well!" The blonde held out a piece of lined paper. "You see how I make my *g*'s? That means I'm very organized. And the way I make my *n*'s and *m*'s, with the loops all scrunched together? That means I have a very warm loving nature. 'Snuggly,' he said."

The women giggled. Huddling over the writing sample, they dropped their voices to excited whispers. "Hedonistic!" exclaimed one. "What the hell does that mean?"

Meeka checked again for Benson, then turned back to the tent. She stared at the sign. Five dollars per analysis. That was less than Eli charged when he worked through his magazine ads, though in this setting it was probably all the market would bear. Still, why was he bothering when he had Benson's hundred thousand?

Unless he'd lost it already. Her stomach twisted at the thought. Her one chance of making peace between the two men was to restore Benson's money. How else could she prove to him that there had been no fraud intended, that money had never been the point of this nonsense?

Eli couldn't have lost it this quickly, she assured herself. Surely he was just doing this for fun or out of habit.

"I told you to wait by the hot-dog stand!" snarled a coarse male voice.

Three glowering bikers loomed over them. Meeka immediately looked down at her shoes, absenting herself from the situation. No doubt these guys were gentlemen and scholars, but, Lord, they looked like trouble!

"We got tired of waiting, Jake," crooned the third woman. She leaned into the speaker and ran a hand up inside his T-shirt. "You wouldn't want me to get *tired*, now, would you?"

He sniggered and hooked an arm around her waist.

"Where's Angie?" demanded another voice, which apparently belonged to a pair of size-fourteen storm-trooper boots.

"Here," said the redhead in a wintry tone. She stalked out of the tent and started away.

The man in the size fourteens tromped after her. Meeka stole a glance under her lashes and saw the man catch Angie by the arm. Then Meeka's eyes refocused just beyond the couple.

Outlined against the advancing thunderheads, a Gypsy-dark woman in a purple and star-spangled robe glided toward the tent. Her two hands glittered with rings, and each hand held a hot dog in a cardboard tray. Beside her trotted Zundi, ears pricked and nose twitching. Suddenly the dachshund leapt for the wieners—her teeth clicked on thin air. The woman laughed and held the hot dogs higher.

"What do you mean, you don't want me to win you a bear?" bellowed Angie's boyfriend, just as the woman in purple came abreast of him.

The redhead shook off his hand. "I changed my mind, Manny, okay?"

"First you gotta *have* a mind before you go changing it," noted the biker. At this witticism, he smirked back at his friends.

"Oh, that's just what he meant!" cried the woman. "You got no respect and you got a wicked short temper." She turned away.

He caught her arm and swung her back. "Short temper? Who the hell says so?" His lantern jaw jutted.

The redhead jerked her thumb toward the tent. "The handwriting guy. Eli the Persi—the Perspicacious, that's who."

"Uh-oh," muttered Meeka.

"Rats!" muttered the woman in purple, who'd just arrived at the tent. She glanced sharply at Meeka, then dove inside.

"What the hell does Eli the Perspi—Perpsi—the Perspiration man know about me?" demanded Manny.

"I showed him your poem," said the redhead. She whipped out the paper, unfolded it and thrust it under the biker's flattened nose. "See where it says 'with your hand on my throttle'? The way you cross your *t*'s? He says that means you're short-tempered."

"You showed him my *poem?*" Manny roared, incredulous.

Meeka jumped as a hand closed on her shoulder from behind. But it wasn't a biker. Cameron Benson scowled down at her. "What's going on?" he growled, nodding toward the bristling couple.

"That poem I wrote *you?*" yelled the mortified poet.

The redhead didn't back down an inch. "That one, yeah, and he said..." Her voice switched to a wicked soprano version of Eli's courtly twang. "He said 'Frankly, my dear, anybody'd who'd compare you to his hawg, then say you were almost as pretty...' well, he said I can do better than that. And he's right. I'm going back to Vinnie!" Dropping the poem at her suitor's feet, she turned and ran.

Manny took two steps after her, stopped, then went back for his poem. "Short-tempered, huh?" he brooded, staring down at it.

"Oh, not you, Manny!" said the bleached blonde, giggling. She was instantly shushed by her boyfriend.

"Well—" Manny crumpled the poem in a ham-size fist "—let's see Eli the Perspiration man analyze this!"

"Eli!" muttered Benson. "Your Eli? He's in there?"

"Yes!" Meeka hissed.

"It figures. Wait out here." Benson shoved through the tent flap.

Meeka followed on his heels. Beyond a table draped with a paisley shawl, the Gypsy woman held up the bottom edge of her tent. Kneeling beside her, Eli was shoving Zundi and his bike saddlebags out through the opening. He looked around, startled. "Meek!"

"Eli Trout?" called Benson. "I'm Cameron Benson, of *American Historic* magazine, and—"

"*Show* me that scum-sucking Eli!" bellowed Manny, erupting into the tent. "Is that him?" Smashing between Benson and Meeka, he headed straight for Eli, hands outstretched.

"Wait your turn!" snapped Benson, catching the back of his belt.

The biker let out a growl and turned, swinging. Benson ducked. "Get out of here!" he yelled at Meeka. Grabbing the biker's wrist, he twisted suddenly. Manny flipped, then bounced off a tent wall, shaking the whole structure. He sat up with a roar of amazement.

Even if she'd been such a coward, Meeka couldn't have fled. The exit was jammed as the two other bikers stormed into the tent. Looking around for a weapon, she saw Madame Gabriella pluck a melon-size crystal ball off the table.

"Be gone, knaves and scuttlebums, or suffer the curse of Madame Gabriella!" shrieked the fortune-teller, brandishing her crystal.

"Ha!" grunted the biker named Jake, making for Benson.

Whipping the shawl off the table, Meeka dropped it over the biker's head. Madame Gabriella cracked the blundering form with her crystal ball, then stepped to the tent entrance. Putting two fingers to her mouth, she blew an earsplitting whistle, then returned to the fray.

Benson threw one biker into another, knocking them both down, and glared at Meeka. "Get out of here, dammit!"

Instead, Meeka turned over the table, blocking the advance of the third biker. Then the tent seemed to be filled with people—a skinny man wielding two wooden juggling bats, a tiny, determined woman with a steaming teapot that commanded instant respect, the carnival policeman and some other tough-looking carnies.

Panting, Meeka backed against a tent wall, then looked around. "Eli?" Kneeling, she lifted the hem of the tent. From this vantage point, she could see all the way down the alley behind the tents. Off in the distance, Eli pedaled his bike toward the edge of the fairgrounds. Meeka scrambled under the tent hem and ran.

CHAPTER NINE

AS SHE RACED for the car park exit, Meeka saw that flickering thunderclouds now covered half the sky. And she wasn't the only one trying to leave. A long line of cars now jammed the exit lane. "Come *on,*" she fumed. By now, Eli would be miles ahead. She turned to check the cars behind her and, a dozen cars back, saw the black Jaguar.

He hadn't been hurt in the brawl, then, if he'd managed to follow her so quickly. But her relief was tempered with exasperation. How would she ever catch Eli with Benson breathing down her neck? If he hadn't identified himself back there in the tent, Eli might not have fled.

On the other hand, if Benson hadn't been there— She jumped as the driver behind her honked. "Okay, okay!" Raindrops spattered the windshield, then the shower intensified. "Wonderful."

But maybe the rain was a blessing in disguise. Eli wouldn't ride far in a downpour. He'd find the first possible hiding place to pitch his tent and he'd go to earth. With any luck, she'd find him and they could go home, see Mr. Finley in the morning. Or even this very night.

By the time Meeka reached the paved road, she'd made up her mind. Eli would have headed for the hills. Turning left, she stepped on the gas.

There were few lights to show the way as she followed the narrow, winding road through Vermont's wooded hills. Eyes wide, she scanned the wall of trees on either side for a cutoff, for knowing he was pursued, Eli would turn off as soon as he could. Her car topped the next rise, and Meeka checked her mirror. A mile behind, she saw two headlights, then four, as a second car swung out from behind the first. Benson, passing someone slower, she'd bet.

Looking ahead, she almost missed the break in the trees, and the car swerved sickeningly on the wet pavement. Then the treads found their grip and she wheeled off the road, through the gap in the trees and onto an unpaved surface.

"Yowp!" The car plunged into a pothole, humped out of it, and Meeka's head brushed the lining above. "Oof!" Logging road, she decided. Not a real road at all. Just what Eli would have been looking for. Stopping the car, she switched off the headlights and turned around. With any luck...

A pair of low-slung headlights sliced past the gap in the trees and vanished up the road. Meeka smiled. She waited a minute more while another set of lights passed by—they belonged to the camper that had delayed the Jaguar. Then she switched on her own lights and chugged up the trail.

It was deeply rutted with the occasional jutting rock, exposed by erosion and frost heaves. Luckily the suspension of her old station wagon was high. Driving no faster than she might have walked, Meeka proceeded, her eyes scanning back and forth. Eli had to be up here, and he couldn't be far ahead.

He might hide, she realized, when he saw her lights coming. He'd have no way of knowing it was her and not Benson—or even the bikers. Rolling down her window, she stuck her head out and yelled, "Eeeli! Eli, it's me!"

She got a face full of rain for her trouble. Sputtering, she rolled the window back up. The car jounced again as it bounded over another rock, and she grabbed the steering wheel with both hands. "Eli, I swear—" A light winked in her rearview mirror. "Uh-oh!"

Downhill, a pair of headlights swung into the gap and bounced slowly after her. Benson. "Don't you ever quit?"

So now what?

Press on regardless, she told herself grimly. She couldn't have turned around if she'd wanted to—branches were brushing both sides of the car. She still had to find Eli—that hadn't changed. *And you're not making it any easier,* she assured her pursuer. Seeing two pairs of headlights coming, Eli would hide for sure.

And if he didn't see their headlights, he'd hear them coming. As it caught up with her, the Jaguar emitted an imperious honk!

"What would you like me to do?" Meeka growled. "Get out of your way?" Her car groaned as it bounced into and over the center rut, then back again.

Benson's horn blasted once more, and his headlights flashed on and off.

"Want me to stop, do you?" But Meeka wasn't in the mood.

The lights in her rearview mirror flashed—on, off, on, off—and he revved his engine, a mechanical roar of displeasure.

"Nobody asked you to follow, did they? Go home to New— Eeep!" Meeka rocked backward in her seat as the Jag nudged her rear bumper. "Cut that *out!*" she yelled, and increased her speed.

The Jag sped up, as well, its lights flashing. "Meeka!"

She could barely hear his shout, over the groans and squeaks of her own car. She shook her head vigorously and kept on driving. "Hey!" she yelped as the Jaguar goosed her back bumper again. "Do that once more and I'll..."

Gritting her teeth, she pressed on, the Jaguar snarling only inches behind, practically shoving her up the mountain. A rock, the tallest she'd come to yet, loomed in her headlights. She swerved to straddle it with her tires.

Miraculously her car cleared it.

But behind her, the Jaguar stopped abruptly. Its headlights bounced upward, then stayed at that unnatural angle.

Oh, Lord! Meeka kept on creeping, her horrified eyes fixed on her rearview mirror.

His lights switched off. The door of the Jaguar swung open, and Benson stepped out into the rain. He slammed shut his door with an impact she could hear over the complaints of her own engine.

Snagged. He'd not seen the rock, following her that closely, and he'd hung himself up on it. Meeka bit her lip as he glanced after her.

He'd never catch her now. She could find Eli, and presuming this road led back to something paved, they could... She stepped on the brakes.

Barely visible in her taillights, Benson crossed his arms and simply stood glaring after her, asking no mercy.

"All right, all right!" Meeka muttered. Bracing herself, she shifted into reverse. He wasn't going to be a happy passenger. Drawing a deep breath, she leaned to unlock his door.

Without a word he swung in and sat, arms folded. Tipping his head back, he glared at the ceiling. Meeka let out her breath and shifted gears again. There was no way to go now but forward. "No way we could get your car off?" she ventured after a hundred yards or so.

"No." The one word quivered with a world of emotion.

And he was blaming her, wasn't he? "If you hadn't been following so close..." she answered his unspoken accusation.

He turned abruptly on the seat. "If *you'd* stopped when I honked—"

"I don't stop for pushy people! *Bumping* me like that—"

"How the devil else was I supposed to get your attention?"

"Who says I have to pay attention to you, Cameron Benson? If you'd just stay out of my life and let me handle this, then—"

"And that's what you're doing, handling this mess, driving up into the middle of God-knows-where in the middle of a blasted rain— Watch *out!*" He grabbed at the wheel. Stone screeched along metal.

"I can drive just fine, thank you, if you'd stop distracting me."

"*Me* distracting *you*!" he snarled, incredulous. But he let go of the wheel and slouched back in his seat. "Where are we going?" he growled after a quarter of a mile. "I presume this is your fallback?"

"Fallback?" She glanced at him, puzzled.

"When you set up an important rendezvous and there's a chance it will be aborted, you set up a fallback. Another place to meet."

Meeka shook her head. "That wasn't a rendezvous back there. I was just looking for Eli and I found him."

"Says you."

"Says me!" she flared. "And now I'm just trying to find him again. No help from you, with all that racket you made, honking and yelling. Uh-oh!"

At the edge of her headlights' range, a mountain brook slashed across the trail. Benson swore while she edged the car closer.

Several boulders formed a stepping path across the current. But what would make a natural bridge for a walker—or a man carrying his mountain bike—made a barrier to a car.

"End of the road," Benson said.

And behind them, the Jaguar blocked their way.

"What is it—five miles back to town?" he added, no doubt thinking the same thing.

Meeka shrugged. "Walk it? In the rain? Not this kid." Automatically she glanced over her shoulder at the mattress that filled the back of the car.

Benson looked, too. "I've slept in worse beds," he said after a moment.

"Do you snore?" she asked warily, though it hardly mattered. With Cameron Benson lying beside her, she wouldn't sleep a wink!

BUT HE DIDN'T SNORE and she had slept, Meeka realized drowsily, when she awoke to the sun shining red through her eyelids. At least, she didn't remember him snoring. Didn't remember anything, past the first hour of lying there, stiff as a board, with the rain rattling cozily on the roof. Eyes shut, she smiled. He'd been just as tense. She'd turned away from him onto her side, and her hip had grazed his thigh. He'd jumped half out of his skin, growled something, then turned his back on her. That was the last she remembered.

Smiling, she snuggled deeper into her pillow, and her mouth brushed something warm. Meeka opened her eyes—found that a large male hand lay curled before her face. That accounted for the warm weight that enfolded her, she realized. They lay spoon-fashion, Benson's arm wrapped around her. Meeka stopped breathing.

To her straining ears, his own breathing sounded deep and regular. Still asleep, thank heavens. The question was whether to slide stealthily away, hoping not to wake him, or to simply lunge for safety? She closed her eyes. This was an important question, one to consider thoroughly, and what better place from which to study it than this delicious, snuggly— She forced her eyes open. *Don't you dare go back to sleep!*

Before her, his hand curled slowly. The tip of his forefinger stroked her lips, and Meeka caught her breath again. After a pause, his finger returned. Aimlessly, it explored the curve of her nose, the softness of her eyelashes.

He's asleep, she reassured herself and, without thinking, closed her lips on his wandering fingertip. He tasted…right.

His arm hardened around her shoulders. "You're awake."

Heat branded her cheeks as she grabbed for the edge of the unzipped sleeping bag that covered them and pulled it up over her head. He'd been awake? Felt her lips close on his finger?

"Come on, sleepyhead, I'm getting stiff." He caught her shoulder and rolled her over to face him. She clutched the bag and brought it with her. Her eyes were watering she was blushing so intensely.

He laughed, a low sexy sound. "Not a morning person, huh?" And tugged the covering down from her face.

As their eyes met, his grin faded. His expression became intent, like a man listening to distant music.

Meeka's mouth formed an O. "Your eye!" It was the color of an award-winning eggplant. She reached to touch it, then realizing how tender it must be, touched his brow instead. Combined with the beard shadow that darkened his jaw, he looked wonderfully rakish, a pirate who'd sailed through a hurricane.

"Bad, huh?" He lifted a strand of hair off her cheek, then held it, rubbing it aimlessly between his fingertips.

"You look like you went ten rounds with a jackhammer." She sat up and twisted away from him. "I've got some ice in the cooler." It was as good an excuse as she was going to get. Still, it took all her willpower to scramble out of their nest, then over the front seat to safety.

"I imagine he looks just as bad," Benson said, sounding annoyed.

Meeka smiled as she found the jeans she'd slipped off the night before and wriggled into them. "I'm sure he does. I'm sure all *three* of them do, but let's put something on that eye." She stepped out of the car into a morning washed clean and shiny as a new copper penny.

While she set up her propane stove on the tailgate of the car and prepared a breakfast of scrambled eggs and ham, Benson washed up in the creek. Raking eggs onto a pair of plates, she looked around. "Benson?"

Returning from across the creek, he spanned the gaps between the boulders with a long-legged litheness that trapped her gaze. She tore her eyes away and poured their orange juice.

"My name's Cameron," he said, looming beside her.

"I know."

"Well, if we're going to sleep together, you might try using it!" He laughed and took one of the plates.

"No 'going to' about it," she said with great precision. She forked up a mouthful of eggs, then glanced up defiantly.

His gaze was laughing, ironic and very, very male, but all he said was, "Cam. Say it."

She couldn't hold that gaze. Cheeks burning, she looked down and muttered, "Cam, then."

While they were putting the cooking gear away, Cam noticed her topographic map. He spread it on the hood and stood frowning down at it. "So this is where he's headed." He traced the dotted line that crossed a stream, then angled around the shoulder of the mountain. "He's making for this town on the other side of the range, isn't he?"

Meeka shrugged. "If he even came this way, that's as good a guess as any."

"He came this way, all right. You can see his bike track in the mud on the far side of the stream. And the prints of his hellhound."

"Gezundheit," Meeka said automatically.

"I didn't—"

"Zundi for short," she translated, grinning.

"It figures." He didn't return her smile, stood staring intently down at her. "He's headed for that town—unless there's a cabin in between?"

He still thought she was aiding and abetting. "Not that I know of," she said brusquely, turning away. "I imagine he camped out last night."

"More fool him," Cam observed, folding the map.

Head high, Meeka opened her door. "He's sixty-three, Cam, even if he doesn't act like it. I don't like him camping in the rain."

He swung into the car beside her. "Meeka, my dear, considering he's got a cool hundred thousand on him, he could have slept at the Ritz. Or hired a dozen Playboy bunnies to hold umbrellas over him all night. I think I'll save my sympathy."

They backed down the long hill in glowering silence. And Cam's temper didn't improve when he inspected his car. "It'll have to be towed," he said grimly.

But apparently mountains limited the range of Cam's car phone. With no way to call for a tow, they had to find their own way around the Jaguar. Luckily Meeka's camping kit included a hatchet for firewood. Cam cleared the brush to one side of his car, and the station wagon squeezed by.

When they reached the main road, Meeka tipped her head toward Bennington and raised her brows.

Benson jerked his chin the other way. "First things first. I'll call a garage after I lay my hands on your uncle."

Meeka glared at him. "And you think I'll help you?"

Cam crossed his arms. His voice went very soft and very polite. "You think you have a choice?"

All the silent way around the mountains, Meeka thought about choices. About Eli in jail. About the ruthless man beside her who wouldn't quit and wouldn't forgive. By the time they'd driven north to the next notch, then south to the town on the east side of the range, she'd made up her mind. Eli needed more help than she and Mr. Finley could give him. It was time to call in an equalizer.

The problem was to get to a phone unobserved. She'd had no chance at their first stop, the town's only general store.

"Old guy on a bike? With a dachshund?" The teenage clerk grinned. "He stopped by here early this morning. Bought a coffee for himself, and a hot chocolate with extra whipped cream for his dog."

"Did he say where he was headed?" Cam asked.

The boy said he hadn't.

They spent the rest of that day together, searching for Eli. It wasn't Meeka's idea, but her suggestion that Cam rent his own car had not been accepted. "I'm out two hundred thousand so far, and you expect me to rent a car?" Looking smugly immovable, Cam had settled into his seat. "Nope. I'm going with you. You know where Eli is headed—"

"I do not!"

"I hope you don't," he'd said, suddenly sober. Then he shrugged. "Anyway, you know how he thinks. That's all the lead I've got."

But Cam had shown himself quite capable of guessing his quarry's thoughts. He'd chosen the same route out of town that Meeka would have chosen—a scenic, windy road that followed a rushing mountain stream, a route sure to attract Eli with his love of pretty views.

Still, they'd found no sign of him. "Must be pushing hard," Cam growled, "that, or we're on the wrong road altogether." He indicated a roadside grocery and gas station. "Pull over. If he rode straight through, he was thirsty by the time he reached here."

That was a good bet. "Skinny old guy with a white mustache?" The woman behind the counter smiled. "Yes. He bought a pound of rice, some fish hooks, two packs of birthday candles, and he pulled a red bandanna out of little Tommy Hurley's ear—or it sure looked like he did, anyway."

"That's him," Cam said grimly. "Did he say where he was headed?"

The clerk didn't think so.

Meanwhile, Meeka chose two sodas from the cooler. She shook her head when Cam reached for his wallet and laid her own bill on the counter.

"He told Tommy he'd better wash out his ears more often," the clerk recalled while she counted out Meeka's change. "I thought Tommy's mother was going to kiss the old guy."

Meeka frowned at the bills the clerk pushed toward her, looked at her sodas, then shook her head. "That's too much. I gave you a ten."

"You— Oh!" The clerk giggled "You did, didn't you? Thanks, I thought it was a twenty."

Outside the store, Cam held out his hand for the keys. "My turn to drive, Meeka, my dear."

As she gave him the keys and a soda, Meeka studied his face. This time his endearment had contained no trace of irony. And he looked happier than he had all morning.

But if something had cheered Cam up, he was no less determined. As they continued upstream, they checked every bank and boulder from which a man might have fished. "But Eli doesn't even like to fish," Meeka felt bound to point out. "He likes fish, but not fishing."

"So why'd he buy hooks?" Cam grumbled.

"Why'd he buy birthday candles?" she countered. "Gezundheit's birthday isn't till November."

Cam gave her a narrow-eyed stare, then sighed. "Let's try this turnoff," was all he said, jerking a thumb toward the river.

It was nearly seven when at last they reached a sizable town. "We'll stop here for the night," Cam decided.

"There's a campground along the river," Meeka said, studying a map. "I'll stay there if they've any sites left."

"There's always a hotel," Cam reminded her with careful neutrality as they passed one.

"Eli forgot to pay me my cut of the swindle," she replied, keeping her voice light. "So I'm on a budget. No hotels."

But though Cam didn't try to change her mind about lodgings, food was another matter. "I've used your car for my own purposes," he announced. "So now I'm buying you supper. No ifs, ands or buts." He parked before an expensive-looking restaurant, told her to order him the biggest steak on the menu, rare, then crossed the street toward a row of shops.

Well, if he had his own private errands, so did she. Meeka ordered their food, then hurried from the table. As she'd hoped, there was a phone in the back hallway near the rest rooms.

She was unable to reach Riley himself when she dialed the number he'd given her. But when she asked his contact if the reporter for *Scoop* was still in Vermont and still interested in the George Washington letter, she was assured that he most definitely was.

"In that case, tell him that Meeka says Eli is alive, and that he was spotted last night." Meeka glanced anxiously toward the dining room. Quickly she gave Eli's last known location and her own whereabouts. "I hope to find him tomorrow. And I'll call Riley when I do. Tell him to remember his promise," she added. "Eli's story in exchange for his help."

She'd barely sat down when Cam joined her. "Bought you something." He set a magazine before her.

George Washington stared glumly from the cover of *Time*. Heroic Traitor? wondered the caption at the bottom of the cover. "Hmm," Meeka murmured in dismay.

While Cam chose a bottle of wine, Meeka scanned the article. Riley had been right. People weren't going to forget about this, and it wasn't going to just fade away. The Daughters of the American Revolution were calling an emergency session. There had been outraged speeches in

Congress. Bumper stickers were popping up all over the nation with the text Say It Ain't So, George!

Pranksters had wrapped the George Washington Monument in toilet paper. "Peter Drysdale," she read aloud. "That's your editor, isn't it?"

"What about him?"

"It says here he's writing a book, a revised history of George's role in the American Revolution. Hopes to have it out later this month."

"An exploitation book," Cam said between his teeth. "The kind creeps crank out whenever there's a major disaster or atrocity. He's fired, in that case." He thumped the table with frustration. "I'm never going to clear George! It's going to be like the Loch Ness monster—against all reason, all *evidence,* people want to believe the worst. Give 'em one bit of nonsense to build a case around and they'll swallow it lock, stock and barrel."

"Is that why you won't release the letter for examination?" she asked. Several congressmen were demanding that apparently.

"It's my responsibility to clear George. My magazine, my responsibility." Cam clenched his jaw while the waiter poured the wine, then added, "You let just any self-appointed authority examine that letter and you'll have chaos. There's real money to be made in championing a conspiracy theory—look at all the books about the Kennedy assassination. Or Marilyn Monroe. That's what Drysdale's doing—cashing in on people's worst instincts. And there'll be plenty of others, if I give 'em half a chance. So, no, nobody examines that letter but my document experts."

Meeka hated to think what a panel of experts must be costing him. "But why's this so important to you, Cam? Clearing George?"

"America's got so many heroes we can spare one like George?" He swirled the wine in his glass and grimaced.

"That was my whole premise when I started *American Historic*. I wanted to say something positive. Wanted to profile all the decent and courageous little people who built this country, the unsung heroes. And now this . . ." He shot her a seething glance. "What are you smiling for?"

Because I like you very very much, Meeka couldn't help thinking, as she shrugged and busied herself buttering a roll. Somebody who could care like that . . . That was rare. Special. But did his caring extend to anything beyond history? Slowly her smile faded.

They changed the topic, apparently of one accord, to anything but history. Cam told her of his trip to Bolivia, of his love of mountain climbing and travel. His father had been a diplomat, and he'd grown up all over the world. "How I got my wanderlust, I suppose." In the candlelight, his eyes were intent, unreadable. "And you, have you never left Vermont?" He'd grimaced when she shook her head. "Never wanted to?"

She laughed huskily. "Never wanted to? I've never seen the ocean, Cam—oh, pictures, sure. I had my wall covered with pictures of the ocean when I was a kid. And icebergs—the colors, all those unearthly shades of green! I've seen them in photos, but that can't be the same as really seeing them?"

"No, it's not the same," Cam said softly. "So why don't you . . ."

She bit her lip and looked down, her eager smile fading. "Well . . . there's Eli. He needs me."

They changed the subject abruptly. To quilts, and how she created her designs from nature, from fairy tales, from dreams. To Cam's plans for his next magazine—one about adventure travel. But now that was on hold till he'd figured out what the present mess would cost him and till he'd found a trustworthy editor for *American Historic* while he started the new project. They'd quickly changed the subject again, then again and again, and had run out of food long before they'd run out of things to talk about.

At last Cam glanced at his watch. "I have some phone calls to make. My secretary has been holding the office together, taking most of this heat. Apparently we're receiving tons of pretty nasty mail." He shrugged and rose. "Wait for me here?"

Meeka shook her head. "I'd like a breath of fresh air, so I'll see you at the car. Could I have the keys, please?"

His hand moved toward his pocket, then stopped. Even by candlelight she could see his face grow wary. "Meeka—"

"Never mind!" She turned on her heel and left before he could refuse. So much for trust! He might be as attracted to her as she was to him, but that didn't change a thing. He still thought she was a crook.

She stalked up and down the sidewalk near the car, trying to mask her hurt with anger. But try as she might, she couldn't blame Cam, not entirely. She had called Riley, after all. They weren't on the same side, much as it felt as if they must be.

"What's *that?*" cried a voice across the street, and Meeka turned. A woman stood pointing, and her companions stared. Meeka stared, too.

Wafting toward them on the warm night breeze was a ghostly, glowing thing. Floating at treetop level, it was silvery, flickering, lumpily globular in shape and utterly silent. If a jellyfish glowed in the dark and flew, it would look like this. "A flying saucer!" shrieked the woman.

"There's another!" yelled a man, who'd stopped his car in midstreet. He pointed to another glowing creature that followed the first.

"UFOs! Call the police!" someone yelled. "*UFOs!*"

Another car stopped. A girl tumbled out and pointed a video camera at the sky.

"Oh, my God, there's another! And there! They're everywhere!" a woman wailed. As if hypnotized, faces raised to the sky, the gathering crowd followed the ghostly, windborne armada. A police car arrived and, blue lights whirling, led the exclaiming parade down the street.

Turning her back on the saucers, Meeka calculated the direction of the breeze—the direction from which the saucers had come—and ran.

Behind her, she heard Cam yell out her name.

Before her, another saucer came ghosting down the wind, attended by its own pointing and hysterical spectators.

"Meeka, blast you, come back here!" Cam shouted.

But she didn't stop and she didn't look back. Eyes fixed on the sky, she headed upwind. For if there was one thing Meeka knew, a fleet of flying saucers meant you were bound to find Star Commander Trout and Lieutenant Gezundheit not very far behind.

CHAPTER TEN

THE TOP OF THE HILL was crowned by a church, its steeple a white finger pointing into the night. Meeka paused there to pant, and Cam caught up with her. "Dammit, Meeka, what's going on?"

She laughed breathlessly and pointed at an elm that stood beside the church. Rustling in the tree's topmost branches, a glowing thing lifted toward the sky, then fell back disconsolately. "I've seen these before."

"Eli!" he said, comprehending. "He's up here?" Taking her hand, Cam hustled her around the church and through a black iron gate into a large graveyard. They paused, scanning the hillside. Nothing moved. The tombstones marched away in pale scalloped rows till they faded into the blackness.

"Eli!" Meeka called. "Eli, if you're up here, will you please, please, come out?"

No one answered.

"If you weren't here..." she complained under her breath.

Cam laughed softly, but not kindly, his lips near her ear. "If I weren't here, he'd probably come out and the two of you would head for the hills! No, thank you." He drew her down a lane of stones toward the white coffin shape of an above-ground tomb. "What's this?"

"This" was a piece of plastic, rustling faintly in the breeze. Several long sticks weighed it down to the marble slab. "A flying saucer," Meeka said, touching the filmy stuff. "It's a dry-cleaning bag. You tie two sticks in a cross and use them to brace the bottom of the bag open. Then you drip some wax and set the candles on the sticks."

"The birthday candles he bought!" Cam remembered. "You light them, the bag fills with hot air, and it rises—I see!" Still holding her hand, he sank onto the slab. "Of all the childish, irresponsible, asinine jokes! That's what your Eli's like? Think of the accidents he could have caused—old people having heart attacks, car wrecks, the cops distracted from real work..."

"That's one way to look at it." Since Cam wouldn't let her go, she sat beside him. "But what about the other way?"

"What other way?" He rested her hand on his knee, set his hand on top of hers and meshed their fingers. "How else can you possibly see it?"

His knee was warm, and she fought the urge to curl her fingers around it. "Maybe Eli scared some people, but he brought a lot of people together, as well. Probably a lot of people who'd never met before."

"The way a neighborhood fire brings people out to rubberneck and mingle?" Cam looked at her cynically.

"Like that exactly! He made something happen—something special and silly that people will smile about for years. The night they left their TV sets, came out of their houses, and chased flying saucers together."

Cam snorted.

"And he gave them a sense of wonder, for a little bit. Didn't you feel it, Cam, when you first saw those things floating? Just the possibility that flying saucers might be real? The wonder of it?"

He snorted again, but his fingers squeezed hers.

"People don't get to feel wonder in their lives very often," Meeka insisted. "But they'll remember this. Eli made them a memory." She glanced down at their clasped hands and her voice grew softer. "And who knows? Maybe two people bumped into each other tonight who ought to have met. Who'd never have met each other at all without Eli's joke."

"Silly romantic—flying saucers as matchmakers!" Cam smoothed his hand up the side of her throat, tipped her head back and kissed her. "George Washington a traitor," he said, laughing. Abruptly his laughter died and he drew back.

They sat staring at each other. "It's a *joke!*" Cam said on a note of outraged comprehension. "He did this all as a sick joke! Wrecked George's reputation! Wrecked my magazine's credibility! The joke meant as much to him as the money, didn't it? I'll kill him!"

"No!" Meeka caught his shoulders. "That's not the way it was!"

"Then how the hell was it?"

"I..." Mr. Finley's image rose before her, his stubby finger pointing. Eli's last-ditch hope, the lawyer had said. "I...I can't talk about it," she said, and swallowed around the ache in her throat.

"Won't," Cam corrected, his voice savage and very soft. "You won't talk about it."

There was nothing more to say. Her sigh said it all. Cam rose, then lifted her to her feet, his hands hard and unfriendly. "Let's go, then."

They stayed that night at a private campground just outside of town. Cam had purchased camping gear during his presupper errands. Working in the grim silence that had enveloped them since leaving the graveyard, he pitched his new tent alongside Meeka's station wagon.

And he still had her car keys, Meeka reminded herself, when she went off to the public showers. He'd probably sleep with them under his pillow! So much for the way they'd talked and laughed at the restaurant.

But it wasn't anger she was feeling as much as sadness. And loneliness—not an emotion she was used to these last few years. Returning from the washroom, her hair and skin deliciously clean from a hot shower, Meeka paused in the darkness outside the radius of their campsite.

Never go to bed angry, her mother had always said.

Easy enough to say! she told herself ruefully, then turned as a light moved in the corner of her eye. Again it flashed, higher this time, and she laughed softly. Lightning bug! She laughed and started after it.

A short while later, hands cupped, she crept toward Cam's tent. A light glowed briefly between her fingers. Kneeling outside the mosquito screen at the opening, she transferred her captive to one hand. With the other, she slid the zipper up. Beyond the two parting halves, she made out Cam's dark head and his shoulders framed by the folds of his sleeping bag. His breathing was deep and even.

Good. Scarcely daring to breath, she placed one hand by his shoulder and leaned into the tent, her cupped hand extended above his head. Opening her fingers, she waited for the firefly to fly.

"What the—" His hand shot up from the darkness.

"Eeep!" His fingers clamped down on her wrist. "Ow!"

His grip gentled, but held. "A good way to get your neck broken, sneaking up on a sleeping man!" he growled.

"I'll remember that." The lightning bug flashed as it crawled on her fingers. "Flying saucer!" she announced. Her voice held laughter even as it trembled—half giggles, half something else entirely. "Here I was trying to scare *you,*" she complained.

He chuckled. The bug crawled down the back of her hand and found Cam's encircling fingers. It glowed again as it started down his wrist. "Lightning bug," he said on a note of wonder. "Haven't caught one of these in years." It flashed again, showing Meeka Cam's face, his eyes fixed on hers.

"Me, neither," she murmured, voice still shaky. "I used to catch whole jarfuls. Let 'em fly around my room at night."

"You, too?" Gently he drew her hand to his chest and held it there.

She swallowed hard, not daring to spread her fingers across his heated flesh, unable to draw away.

The firefly flashed. Cam's other hand twined through her dangling hair. "You're wet."

"Had a shower." As he had before he'd gone to bed. His skin smelled clean, with a trace of soap.

He moved her hand to his cheek—its roughness scratched deliciously against her palm. With a tiny moan, she cupped her fingers to his chin.

"Meeka." He tugged her hair, bringing her face down to his.

The bug flashed and flew to alight on the tent wall. Her breath was coming ragged. She could feel Cam's on her cheek, hot and quicker than her own. "Don't kiss me."

The bug flashed. "Why not?" His voice caressed her.

She felt as if she was falling from a very great height. That she must complete the fall. "Because you think I'm a . . . a crook."

"No." Letting go her hand, he touched her lips with his fingertips. "No. I . . . judge people by the little things, my dear. That's where you find the truth. You could have kept that money today back at the store, when the clerk gave you the wrong change." His fingers roamed her face, tracing her eyebrows, fingering her earlobe, outlining its delicate whorls.

"Ohh . . ." she almost sang, half hypnotized by the sensation.

Releasing her hair, his other hand sought the arm on which she leaned. Hard fingers encircled her wrist, smoothed up its damp bareness, then down again, restless, caressing. "I don't think you're a crook at all, Meek. I think you're loyal to a crook."

She moaned a tiny dissent and shook her head. Her hair brushed his face. His hand tensed on her arm, then wandered on. The firefly gleamed. "I can understand why you'd be that loyal," Cam murmured hoarsely, "the way he took you in as a kid." His fingers stroked her shoulder, moved across her T-shirt, found the hollow below her throat. "But Meeka, it's time to grow up, time to see Eli for what he really is, time to move on."

"I..." It was so hard to say, with her heart hammering the way it was. She could hardly speak at all, but still, she had to say it. "I *do* see him clearly. It's you..."

"Meek." Cam's hand returned to her hair and took hold. "I don't want to argue with you tonight." Gently he tugged, urging her downward. "I want to make love with you."

She let out a little shivering sigh. "You, who are going to put Eli in jail?"

The gentle pull ceased, though still he held her. "I may."

The firefly flashed, showing her Cam's unreadable eyes. "Suppose I...let you make love to me, if you wouldn't send him to jail..."

His hand clenched in her hair, hurting her, but she didn't cry out. "Is that what you're offering?"

She breathed in, then out, three slow times before she shook her head. "No...I... No, I can't do that." But oh, she wanted to!

And saving Eli would just be the excuse! she realized in a flash of the firefly's light.

"Good," he growled, and let her go. "'Cause I couldn't take you on those terms if you did." Lifting her other hand from his chest, he kissed it, then pushed it aside. "So get the heck out of here and let me sleep—if I can."

Meeka had retreated to the car and crawled into her sleeping bag before her brain really started to function again. But when it did, she smiled slowly, stretched a luxurious catlike stretch. And fell asleep.

To say Cam was grumpy the next morning was to put it mildly. Meeka didn't mind. Nothing could touch her own mood. She wanted to smile over the silliest things.

Once they'd showered and changed, she into fresh clothes that she'd packed for the trip, Cam into the blue shirt and jeans he'd purchased along with his camping gear, she'd offered to cook breakfast. But there Cam dug in his heels. He wanted coffee, not that herbal tea mouthwash she preferred, and he wanted pancakes. They'd eat out. "My treat," he snapped when she tried to protest.

By his fourth cup of coffee, Cam's mood had improved, though Meeka caught him studying her with an odd, brooding look each time she looked up from the newspaper she'd purchased.

Cup in one hand, he leaned over the map of Vermont he'd spread out on the table. "Do you think he'll stay put or move on?"

Meeka bit her lip. *Whose side am I on?*

When she didn't speak, Cam's face darkened. "If he heard you calling at the graveyard last night, he didn't come out," he reminded her. "Which means he may have spotted me. If so, then he knows I'm still on his tail."

Meeka shrugged her eyebrows. "Makes sense."

"Even if he doesn't know, he caused a panic in town last night." Cam nodded at her copy of the local paper, where a front-page photo showed a "saucer" fluttering down toward a policeman, who stood his ground with drawn pistol. "And apparently Eli doesn't stick around to own up to his mistakes."

"He doesn't like trouble," Meeka admitted. "He's rather shy actually."

Cam choked on his coffee. "Shy? Setting the whole damned country on its ear? I'll give him shy!"

Meeka buried her nose in her paper. But Cam was right. Below the lead story on the saucer hoax, a syndicated feature from a news service concerned George Washington's early attempts to secure a commission in the British Army, during the French and Indian War. A sidebar was devoted to the world-renowned document analyst, who headed Cam's panel of experts. The man was famous for discovering historical forgeries.

"I think he'll move on," Cam concluded. "You said he can't sit still for long. But my bet is he's tired. Clearly he's in great shape to have made it so far, but he's sixty-three. So today he'll choose a paved road over a mountain trail." Cam consulted the map. "I've got two probables—at least they're the roads I'd choose if I were wandering. One leads up past a ski resort. The other follows the river. Which would you guess?"

Without looking up from her reading, Meeka shrugged.

Cam caught the top edge of the page and pulled it down. "Meek?"

She sighed. "The river. Eli hates skiing."

"Because of your father?"

She blinked. "I never thought— Maybe that *is* why."

"Thanks," Cam said softly.

Their eyes held, and it was last night all over again. Cam's hand slid slowly across the table toward hers.

"Ms. Ranier?"

They both jumped and glanced sideways. Riley, the reporter for *Scoop* magazine, stood beaming beside them. He offered his hand to Meeka. Automatically she took it.

"So good to see you again," he said, eyes twinkling. "I wonder if you'd care to join us?" His pointed chin indicated a table across the room.

Meeka turned to look and found herself meeting the wounded bull-moose glare of Justin Hawthorne. Her mouth dropped.

"No, she doesn't care to join you," Cam said flatly. "What are you doing here?"

"Seeking an interview with this young lady's uncle," Riley admitted cheerfully.

"Might be difficult," Cam observed, "since he's dead."

Chuckling, Riley released Meeka's hand. "If you really think that, Mr. Benson, then you're sadly behind the times! Read my latest article. It'll be out in this afternoon's edition. Front page, of course."

"How—" Cam bit off the question. His eyes flicked to Meeka's pinkening cheeks.

"You're sure you won't join us?" Riley asked again.

"Anything you have to say, you say here," Cam insisted.

Riley gave an amiable shrug. "Very well. I wondered if Meeka knew that your foremost expert witness declared the letter genuine late yesterday?"

"He did?" Meeka squeaked, turning to stare at Cam. Cam had called his secretary last night. Surely she would have told him.

"How the hell did..." Cam took a deep breath. "That was a confidential and exclusive analysis. For my eyes only."

Riley beamed. "*Scoop*'s name is no idle boast." His gaze returned to Meeka. "If Benson didn't tell you, then perhaps he also forgot to tell you that, rather than accepting that verdict, he's waiting for the rest of his panel to report in, in the hope they'll tell him what he wants to believe."

"Get out of here," Cam said so softly it was almost inaudible. His fingers curled into fists on the tabletop, then splayed out flat and stiff.

Riley backed up a step. "Surely." He gave Meeka a speaking glance. Then he turned and left.

"Your expert said..." It was just beginning to hit Meeka. "You knew this last night, didn't you, after you'd called—"

Cam threw a bill onto the table and stood. "It doesn't change a thing." Catching her arm, he started toward the door.

"It does!" Because there was no way Cam could prosecute Eli if he couldn't prove the letter false.

"We'll discuss it in the car, shall we?"

But Riley caught up with them out in the parking lot. Cam had already slid behind the wheel and Meeka had opened her door. "Meeka?" The reporter materialized at her shoulder. "I thought you might like this—a copy of my article that comes out this afternoon." He handed her several typewritten pages. "Any news of him?" he hissed.

"Here last night," she muttered. "Maybe biking north on the river road. That's where we're trying, anyway. Why are you with Justin Hawthorne?"

Riley winced elaborately. "I needed someone to identify Eli. Don't worry, I'll be only too pleased to ditch him as soon as he's served his purpose. Why are you with Benson? I told you not to trust him."

But Cam had stepped out of the car and was now rounding the hood with unmistakable determination. "Stay in touch!" Riley hissed. He set off at a deceptively casual stroll toward his own car across the parking lot.

"Scum!" Cam said. He transferred his glare to the paper Meeka held. "What's that?"

In the end, Meeka drove while Cam read Riley's article. Though he said not a word, she could judge his mounting rage by the acceleration in his breathing. But that was all right—she was furious, too.

"Garbage," Cam said finally, and ripped the pages in two.

Meeka grabbed for them. "I wanted to read that!"

"Oh, I can tell you what it says." Cam tossed the article onto the floor. "I'm the villain of the piece—that is, George and I are the villains. Riley implies that I'm trying to have things both ways. First I made millions—" he let out a bark of bitter laughter "—millions by publishing George's treachery in my magazine.

"And now that I've made my profits smearing George, I want my purchase price back. So now I'm claiming the letter's a forgery. And in my efforts to prove the letter false, I'll stop at nothing. Apparently I drove your uncle, a 'gentle historical buff and dealer in antique documents,' to attempt suicide. And now I'm doing my dastardly best to suppress the evidence that George Washington was indeed a traitor. I've muzzled my own expert witness now that he's certain the letter is genuine."

"Well, haven't you?" Meeka demanded. "You knew last night and you never told me."

"I didn't muzzle him well *enough* apparently, damn his eyes!"

"And now you're ignoring his verdict?" Meeka scowled.

"Because he's an idiot, for all his credentials!" Cam glared out the window. "Where'd the river go? Are we on the right road?"

"Don't change the subject. How can you not believe your own experts?"

"Expert. He's just the first of a five-man panel."

"The second, counting Drysdale's man. *Two* experts say it's genuine."

"I don't care if it's two hundred! George never did it. And tell me, please, just how did that scumbag find out Eli didn't drown?"

Meeka clenched her hands on the wheel. "I told him."

"Stop the car," Cam said softly.

Drawing a breath, Meeka pulled over to the shoulder. "Yes?"

"You're dealing with the scum of the earth, a reporter from *Scoop*. Do you realize that? Of all the intellectually dishonest, low-minded, rumor-mongering—"

"Intellectually dishonest! Who's ignoring his own experts? *You're* the one suppressing evidence! You *want* to send Eli to jail!"

"No!" Cam slammed the dash with his palm. "I want to clear George." Swinging around, he caught her shoulders. "I...want...to...clear...George." He gave her a tiny shake. "And I'm not suppressing evidence. I'm suppressing opinion."

A bead of sweat trickled between her breasts. She was hot all over, as if she'd come running to this confrontation. "So—it's opinion if it goes against you! If your expert had come out on George's side, you'd have called it evidence quick enough!"

He shook her again, though it was more a rocking motion, as if he couldn't decide whether to draw her to him or toss her backward through her open window. "Because I know better." His thumbs moved across her upper arms, and he rocked her again. "Tell me something. Do you honestly—honestly—believe that George wrote that letter?"

Meeka opened her mouth, then closed it again. She was too hot already. Now she could feel her blood rising in a slow inexorable tide. "I'm...not at an expert," she hedged. "It doesn't matter what I think."

He rocked her so close that their noses touched. "Oh, yes, it does. I'm beginning to think that's all that matters."

She wished that were so! She dared not let him see *how* she wished that were so. Twisting aside, she stared through the windshield, panic and something like laughter fluttering in her chest.

"Meek?" he said huskily.

He couldn't have meant what she thought he meant. It shouldn't matter even if he had. A man who'd send Eli to jail, who'd stop at nothing to catch him... "You're right," she said breathlessly, "we've lost the river."

He pulled her close, kissed her ear and let her go. "So we have," he said matter-of-factly. "Where's the map?"

Somewhere in their argument, they'd taken a wrong turn. They ended up cutting cross-country on an unpaved road, then going miles out of their way to find a bridge over the river. They kept their conversation carefully businesslike, their eyes off each other—as if each of them had said more than intended and now regretted it. Once they'd returned to the river road, they followed it for miles until it ended at a highway.

"Would he ride along this?" Cam asked, scanning the expanse of elevated concrete with its whizzing traffic.

Meeka shook her head. "Eli doesn't believe in highways. And Zundi despises trucks—chases 'em. She wouldn't sit still in her basket for this."

"So he didn't come this way," Cam concluded. "That explains why nobody noticed him at any of the stores we tried."

So they had cut cross-country again to intersect their other choice of the morning, the road that passed the ski resort. They retraced that route all the way back to the day's starting point—without finding one sign of Eli.

By then the sun was setting. So they ate in the same restaurant, talked again of anything and everything under the sun except their quarry until the kitchen closed and the head waiter turned them out. Then they pitched their camp in the same campground.

But this time Meeka left the fireflies alone.

CHAPTER ELEVEN

"SO NOW WHAT?" Meeka asked as they finished breakfast in what she was starting to think of as *their* restaurant. She touched the unfolded map on the table between them. "That road maybe?"

Shaking his head, Cam spread thumb and forefinger to bracket an inch of map. "We missed about four miles of our first road yesterday. See? Here's where we lost the river, at this fork. And we didn't find the road again till we crossed this bridge. So we never covered this stretch."

The section they'd missed the day before was only a few miles from town. Two miles down it, Cam slowed the car. "Ah."

A life-size plywood cutout of a llama with a Mona Lisa smile and a daisy chain painted around its neck, stood next to a battered mailbox.

Llaughing Llama Farm proclaimed the letters painted on the llama's side. LLama Treks, Yarn and Photo Opportunities. Welcome!

"If Eli passed this way, he stopped here," Cam declared. "Anybody who could spell 'laughing' with two *l*'s..."

"...is Eli's kind of person," Meeka agreed as he turned down the drive toward the distant farmhouse.

But if Eli had stopped by the day before—or even the night before that, the night he'd launched his saucers—the place had an air of emptiness today. No car sat in the driveway before the house. Nor did there seem to be a vehicle near the barn. Still, Meeka was brought up short with delight. The delicate tips of their long ears nearly touching, three llamas leaned over the fence to study their visitors.

"They're not laughing," Cam observed. He bounded up the front steps to the porch, lifted his hand to knock on the door, then paused. A poster had been tacked to the peeling clapboards beside the front door. "Looks like Riley beat us to this one."

But Meeka was staring at the poster in horror. It was a photo of Eli grinning broadly below his bushy mustache. Wanted! the caption proclaimed. Reward $2000.

"'For information leading to the apprehension of Eli Trout,'" she read in a stunned voice, "'suspected forger of the George Washington letter'!" She turned fiercely on Cam. "Did you—"

"Don't be absurd." He touched a smaller line of print. "The reward's being offered by the Green Mountain Sons of Liberty—who the devil are they? 'Anyone with information should contact Justin Hawthorne,'" he read. "Ah—the historical fascist. Riley's pal."

"Yes," Meeka agreed numbly. Below the plea for information leading to Eli's capture, a line separated the poster into upper and lower halves. The lower headline announced that a historic revolutionary war battle would be reenacted this weekend at the Fourth of July Mountain Muster near Middlebury, all proceeds of which would finance the bounty on Eli. "But why do you think it was Riley that posted this?" Her eyes flicked to the business card Cam was tapping. It had been tacked to the wall on top of the poster.

"Better yet, contact me," Riley had printed neatly on his business card. "I'll pay $4000 for the same information."

"But Hawthorne and Riley were traveling together," Meeka protested.

"Doesn't mean they aren't working at cross-purposes," Cam observed dryly. "Witness the two of us. You told him to try this road?"

"Yes," she confessed in a very small voice.

"Some friend." Cam started down the steps.

I don't know who Eli's and my friends are anymore, she thought unhappily as she followed him toward the barn. Justin Hawthorne certainly wasn't one. And Riley? Well, Riley had claimed he was only using Hawthorne, and piggy-backing his own note on top of Hawthorne's poster was surely one way to use him.

But did she and Eli need a user for a friend? Cam would never use someone behind his back.

Ahead of her, Cam rattled the barn door, found it locked, then stopped to read a note that was thumbtacked to its surface. "Joey, you're fired!" the note declared. But its author had apparently had second thoughts, for that line was crossed out.

"Okay, you're not fired," the message continued, "but this is your absolutely LAST chance. I've found someone else to help me do the home in Middlebury. And since you're not coming along, I'll stay overnight with friends. So please bring everyone into the barn tonight and let them out no later than eight tomorrow. I'll be back by ten without fail." It was signed "Jane."

"I wonder who she found to help her?" Cam mused. His chin lifted.

Meeka turned to follow his gaze and laughed in surprise. The three llamas were galloping in single file toward the road. Suddenly, in perfect unison, they stopped short, bunched their four feet, and bounced skyward as if attached to pogo sticks, their elegant ears flopping ludicrously. "What on *earth* are they—"

A rusty black pickup truck came rolling up the drive. The two llamas riding in back, chins propped on the cab of the truck, surveyed their mates with suave disdain.

"Hello!" A woman with pale, frizzy blond hair and a wide smile called as the truck rolled past to park before the barn.

The bed of the truck was fenced in with steel mesh to contain its passengers. Below the tailgate, a red bumper sticker pleaded Say It Ain't So, George!

"A woman after my own heart," Cam murmured as she slid from the truck.

Clad in snug, well-worn blue jeans and a checked shirt, she looked like a teenager. But as she approached, Meeka realized she was decades older. Her shoulder-length hair was a fluffy blend of silver and pale gold, and a web of laugh lines edged her vivid blue eyes. "Hello, I'm Jane Rice. Have you been waiting long?"

"Not very," Cam assured her as they shook hands.

They stood back while Jane climbed into the bed of the truck to untie her llamas. "Were you looking for a llama trek?" she asked, holding a lead and waiting while the cream-colored, spotted llama dithered, then leapt to the ground. Nimble as a cat, the dark brown llama followed.

"Actually we were looking for information," Cam said.

Jane's small body seemed to stiffen. "Oh," she said too casually. Jerking into motion, she turned to Cam and handed him the lead of the spotted llama. "Here, would you hold Pizarro?" She led the other animal toward a gate that led into the pasture.

"He's gorgeous!" Hand outstretched, Meeka approached Cam's charge. "Do you think he bites?"

"No," Cam said, "but don't touch his head. Llamas don't like that." Indeed, though its cloven hooves remained planted, the llama leaned away and averted its head, reminding Meeka of an eight-year-old boy shrinking from a maiden aunt's kisses. "You can pet his shoulder, but they're not very cuddly."

"You know llamas, then," Jane observed, returning to take his lead.

"I've met a few in the Andes." Hands in his pockets, Cam wandered toward the truck. Meeka was allowed to admire the pack animal before its owner led it away.

"We're trying to catch up with a friend of ours," Cam said when she returned. Eyes fixed on her face, he described Eli.

"I've never met anyone of that description," Jane Rice said briskly. Her earlier warmth had cooled considerably. "Now if you don't want a trek, I've been away all night and I've got lots of chores."

"You've never met such a man?" Cam challenged. He jerked his chin toward the pickup's cab. "You have a photo of him in your truck."

A wave of scarlet washed across her face, then ebbed. "That poster? I got that in Middlebury. Men dressed in revolutionary-war uniforms are tacking 'em to everything but the cars and the cows."

"But why bring one home with you?" Cam inquired silkily.

"Two thousand dollars—that's quite a reward," the woman insisted. "I could use..." Her voice trailed away and she shrugged. "Haven't seen him."

Cam reached into the truck, lifted something off the seat and turned. "Eli didn't give you these fish hooks?"

"I..." Her face reddened again. "Yes, he gave them to me," she admitted, her voice defiant. "He was hungry, but he found he couldn't bear to fish." She snatched the container and held it two-handed, her thumbs stroking its surface. "So he gave them to me, said they'd make good hangers for Christmas-tree ornaments." A very private smile flickered across her face, then vanished. "And he cleaned out my barn and I let him sleep there. I fed him and his dog supper, then breakfast, and then they went on their way. Satisfied? Now get out of here." She jerked a thumb toward the road.

"I'm Eli's niece," Meeka said quickly.

"You're Meeka?" The woman searched her face.

Eli told her about me! Meeka nodded, biting back a delighted grin.

"So who's your grizzly bear?" Jane tossed her head at Cam.

Meeka laughed. "Publisher of *American Historic,* the magazine that bought the letter. He doesn't think George did it."

"Neither do I." Jane turned to Cam. "But Eli didn't tell me anything at all about that. I guessed he was on the lam from something, but I didn't see this poster until after he left me in—until after he left." Stepping closer, she poked a slender finger at Cam's chest. "But I *will* tell you this. Whatever he did, whatever he's done, it was done honorably. With no intention of hurting anyone. I'll stake my last llama on that!"

"And you're such a good judge of character?" Cam said.

"I taught high-school English for twenty-five years before I decided to make my fortune in llamas," Jane said, her laugh lines deepening with self-mockery. "I'm an excellent judge of character."

Cam nodded. "And you drove him and his bike to Middlebury, where he helped with your llamas at some sort of home. Then you left him there."

"No! I didn't say—" She stopped and clenched her hands into fists.

"Excellent judge of character, terrible liar," Cam observed, dropping an arm around Meeka's shoulders. He started her toward the car.

"Please don't hurt him," Jane called after them. "He didn't say what he was running from, but I could tell he was scared to death."

"Good!" Cam retorted. "He should be."

Meeka rolled down her window, as he turned the car around. "Can I come back and visit sometime?" she called.

Jane gave her a wavering smile, then nodded. As they drove off, she stood there, a small figure growing tinier in the distance. "Another lovely lady on the wrong side," Cam murmured, glancing back in his mirror. "What's that blasted old geezer got?"

"He's Eli." Meeka lifted her arm just before Jane vanished beyond the trees.

It was midafternoon by the time they reached Middlebury. "First thing to do is find the home where Jane took her llamas," Cam said as they drove down its tree-shaded streets. "Nursing home?"

"Veterans' home?" Meeka countered. "Oops!" She pointed at a tree they were passing. "There's another of Hawthorne's posters."

They'd seen them posted along every roadside in almost every town through which they'd driven. "Hawthorne and his men must be blanketing the state!" Cam growled. "Why does that jerk have to be on my side?"

And why can't you be on mine? Meeka thought.

She bit her lip as they passed another poster. The poster hadn't specified that Eli was wanted dead or alive, but what if somebody jumped to that conclusion?

"What's a mountain muster, anyway?" Cam wondered aloud.

Meeka made a face. "It's where a bunch of historical reenactors muster, or meet, and camp out together for a weekend. Justin Hawthorne organizes one somewhere in the state every Fourth of July. I imagine he's adding this special battle reenactment on top of something he'd planned months ago. What are we stopping for?" she added as Cam pulled up before a convenience store.

"To check a phone book," he said.

Minutes later, he strode out of the store, a grim smile hardening his face. He tossed a newspaper into her lap. "Closing in."

A photo on page one showed a man and a woman leading two llamas up a staircase while several people in wheelchairs looked on. The man who led Pizarro was Eli of course, and his companion was Jane Rice. At Jane's heels,

Zundi humped her way up the steps, her ears lifted like furry wings. Llamas Cheer Rest Home Residents proclaimed the caption.

Meeka sighed and studied Eli's face. He looked thinner than when she'd seen him last, if that was possible. But his angular face was half turned toward Jane, his lips parted as if the camera had caught him in mid-joke.

And if they were closing in, so was everyone else, they realized when they reached St. Cecelia's Nursing Home. "Where the man in that picture went?" The woman behind the reception desk bristled. "If I had a dollar, mister, for every time I've been asked that question in the last twelve hours! The *New York Times* wants to know where he went! So do '60 Minutes' and the 'Today Show'! And you know what?" She stuck out her chin. "I... don't... know."

She took a breath and went on, "He walked out that door with the llamas and Miss Rice, and that's the last we saw of him. But he's welcome back anytime. We don't care if he did prove that Washington was a traitor."

A sweet-faced old woman in a wheelchair had rolled herself up to the desk to hear this diatribe. "That's right!" She nodded wholehearted agreement. "Any man who can get old Mr. Duncan to put in his teeth and play 'K-K-K-Katy, beautiful Katy' on a comb is all right in our book. That old coot hasn't smiled in twenty years— Mr. Duncan, I mean."

"So now what?" Meeka asked once they'd made their escape.

Cam glowered at a wanted poster of Eli tacked to the tree nearest their car. "First, food and some phone calls."

Since there was only one phone at the restaurant, they took turns. Meeka could feel Cam's eyes drilling into her back while she made her call to Beth. "Hi, it's me!" she said.

"Meek! About time you called," Beth yelped. "Where are you? They've all found out Eli's alive, did you know that? Seth Harkness drove through Middlebury yesterday, and there was a picture of Eli with a llama, of all things, plain as day! On the front page of their paper! Seth brought it back and tried to collect the bounty Justin Hawthorne is offering. But he couldn't find Hawthorne anywhere. And all the reporters saw the photo when he stopped by the Coffee Pot, and they just *stormed* out of town, thank God for that! And Delbert Henley is so mad at Eli for being alive he plans to bill him for dragging the lake. He says he hopes Justin Hawthorne and his Sons of Liberty shoot Eli and save him the trouble."

"Oh, great!" Meeka muttered when Beth stopped for breath.

"And Eli sent you a postcard," Beth swept on. "It's written in a sort of pig latin with hiccups, but Ric figured it out. It says he's out of money and that he needs you to meet him tomorrow—the Fourth—and bring him some money, or at least bring him some food. Preferably fried chicken, or if you can't manage that, then ham sandwiches with pickles and potato chips. He must be starving. He sounds like you and me when we used to make up dream meals in Miss Wiggly's seventh-period math class."

"Where does he—" Meeka was suddenly aware that Cam was leaning on the wall beside her. "Uh...where?" she muttered, then scowled as Cam caught the phone and leaned close to listen, his temple touching hers.

"Where?" Beth repeated. "Oh—where does he want you to meet him?"

"Uh, Beth—" But Cam pressed a finger to her lips.

Beth was past stopping, anyway. "That's the problem! Ric hasn't a clue! The postcard says July the Fourth at the turkey's recycled shoot."

"That's all it says?" Cam demanded.

"That's all it—" Beth stopped short. "Who's that?"

"Turkey's recycled shoot," Cam mused after he'd finished a cordial chat with Beth and hung up the phone. "That mean anything to you?"

Mutely Meeka shook her head.

Cam caught a lock of her hair and tugged meditatively. "Would you tell me if it did?"

She shrugged. She just didn't know anymore.

He gave her hair a slightly sharper tug, then punched a series of numbers into the phone. Meeka stayed beside him. If he could eavesdrop on her conversations, then she'd darned well listen to his!

But the conversation was cryptic, and the answer left Cam scowling. "What?" she demanded when he'd hung up the phone.

"That was Hardy—you might say he's second in command on my panel of experts. The remaining four had promised they'd reach a verdict on the letter's authenticity by this afternoon. But now they want more time to repeat some of the tests and to think about it. He says it'll be tomorrow before they can say."

"And if they think the letter's authentic?" she pressed him.

"They won't." He started for the exit.

"If they do, Cam?"

"I don't want to think about it. Do we even have a country without George? What do the past two hundred years mean if we were founded by a traitor? Let's start by canceling the Fourth of July." He opened the door for her.

"But if they do?" she repeated, smiling up at him as she passed. He couldn't do anything to Eli if he couldn't prove the letter was a forgery! And if Cam couldn't hurt Eli, then...

"Don't get your hopes up," he said roughly, dropping an arm across her shoulders as he fell into step. "If you want to think about something, think about where we're sleeping tonight. It's past six."

That was too close to what she'd been thinking. As he noted her reddening cheeks, his arm tightened, but he looked away quickly. "I vote for that place," he said, his voice supremely casual. He nodded at a lovely old inn with soaring chimneys and overshadowing elms, which stood just across the road. "Looks like the kind of place that would have a big four-poster bed with mountains of down pillows."

"Two four-poster beds," she said, refusing to look at him.

But he swung her around to face him. "*One* would do nicely, Meeka." He stood very still, his arm neither forcing her closer nor letting her go.

She could feel, quite distinctly, her heartbeat—in the tips of her fingers, in her ears, thundering in her breast. It would be so easy to close the distance between them, and it made more sense than anything she'd ever known. And yet... "And Eli?"

Slowly Cam shook his head. "No bargains, my dear. This is you and me."

And yet Eli was part of her, too. Eli, who'd apparently lost or spent every penny of Cam's money, if he had no way to buy food, had Cam thought of that? Of course he had. He was always two jumps ahead of her. But how could she ever make peace between them? Ever convince Cam that this had all been a foolish accident if she couldn't restore his money? With a weary sigh, she leaned her forehead against Cam's chest.

He dropped his face into her hair. "Meek?"

She sighed and shook her head against him. "I can't!" she whispered. "Not while you— I just can't, Cam."

He stood very still. Then his cheek brushed across her hair as he nodded. "Okay." His voice held no emotion. "Then let's go get Eli and be finished with this damned idiocy."

She looked up, astonished. "You know where he is?"

"No, but I know where he'll be."

CHAPTER TWELVE

AS THEY DROVE toward the mountains, the sinking sun painted the landscape in long shadows and swaths of ruddy gold. "Where are we going?" Meeka asked finally.

"If Beth received that card today, then Eli mailed it yesterday," Cam said. "So he must have sent it after he left Jane and the nursing home. And after he'd seen the posters plastered all over Middlebury."

"Yes, and so?"

"You're to meet at the 'turkey's recycled shoot.' At a turkey shoot."

"Eli doesn't like hunting any more than he likes fishing!" Meeka protested.

"But would you say—or would Eli say—that Justin Hawthorne's a bit of a turkey? That's how he strikes me." Cam cocked an eyebrow her way.

"Yes! Eli can't stand—" And suddenly she remembered the words in Henry Calloway's note, the day this disaster had started.

Sure seemed a shame to waste the letter on a stuffed turkey like Justin Hawthorne!

"A turkey shoot! Justin Hawthorne's battle reenactment?"

"A recycled battle," Cam translated, nodding. "Though, as a historian, I'm damned if I can think of any revolutionary-war battle that occurred in this part of the state."

"Oh, that's easy!" Meeka giggled. "That's what drove Eli crazier than anything. Sometimes they reenact battles that never happened!"

Cam threw back his head and laughed. *"What?"*

"They do!" She chortled. "Since there weren't enough real battles in Vermont to reenact, Hawthorne and his men do fake reenactments."

"Battles that should have happened if all had gone right with the world!" Cam grinned. "I'm beginning to see why Eli can't stand the guy."

"But you really think that's what Eli meant?"

"I'd have bet on this without the postcard," Cam affirmed. "It's close enough—less than twenty miles away from where he was last seen. And it's being held in his honor—the admission fee pays his bounty. It would be as good as attending your own funeral. Do you think he could resist?"

Shyly Meeka reached out and rubbed her knuckles along Cam's arm. "You're starting to know him," she said softly.

The mustering place was an upland meadow at the edge of the Green Mountain National Forest. An unpaved track led uphill to a pasture filled with parked cars. "Beautiful," Cam murmured.

A hundred yards above the cars, and two centuries back in time, rows of army tents patterned the rich green of the hillside. In contrast to the dark forest that edged the mountain's shoulder, their white canvas sides glowed rose red in the sunset. A woman in a long calico skirt and a boy in buckskins trudged up the hill from the car park, their arms loaded with blankets and bundles.

In the distance, other figures moved among the tents. Their clothes were the muted shades of leather and butternut, indigo and animal fur, with random splashes of military scarlet or black.

"Look at the tepees!" Meeka pointed. The larger cone-shaped tents were pitched off to one side of the main encampment. Camp fires flickered and plumes of smoke rose toward the deepening sky.

"And looks like we've got company," Cam murmured as two men holding muskets stepped forward to intercept the car.

A man dressed in the uniform of a colonial soldier leaned down to look in Cam's window. "Evening, folks! What can we do for you?"

"Thought we'd have a look around," Cam said easily.

A man dressed in fringed buckskins, the fur of some large shaggy animal tied across his back, peered in Meeka's window. "'Fraid tonight's not for tourists," he said apologetically. "Just for folks who came in period dress."

Meeka gave him her best smile. "Late twentieth century won't do?"

The mountain man showed tobacco-stained teeth that seemed all too historically correct. "'Fraid not, ma'am. We're talking 1700s to 1840s, tonight. Fur trappers and traders to Andy Jackson. But come back tomorrow and we'll sure put on a show for you. Everybody's invited to the battle."

"Ten sharp," the soldier chimed in. "But come before that if you want to look around and see us burn the effigy."

"The effigy?" Cam repeated.

"The effigy of that damned traitor, Eli Trout. We're offering a bounty on the skunk. But till we lay our hands on him, we might as well burn his effigy—'60 Minutes' is going to film it."

Ka-pow!

Uphill, a volley of gunfire rang out, then echoed dully off the mountainside. A cloud of white smoke rose, then beneath it, a tiny figure lowered the American flag that flew before one of the army tents.

"So if you'd excuse us, folks," the mountain man ended delicately.

While Cam turned the car around, the colonial sauntered back to intercept another car packed full of historically incorrect people.

"Peterson of the *Times,*" Cam noted, stepping on the gas.

"And friends!" added Meeka. "How did they figure it out?"

"Maybe they haven't. But they followed the trail as far as Middlebury, and what else is there to cover if they can't find Eli himself? They've got to be desperate for news by now."

"So they'll be here tomorrow for the battle, as well," she concluded.

"Yup. Looks like it's shaping up to be some party."

They ended up staying in a private campground, some five miles back toward town. As they pitched their camp, then fixed a quick snack on the stove, neither of them was inclined to talk. Then they both set off for the showers.

When she came out of the women's side, washed and ready for bed, Meeka spotted Cam. He was inside the camp's phone booth, receiver tucked between ear and shoulder, his face grim.

She returned to their camp and sat at the picnic table, her eyes fixed on the snowdrift of stars overhead. What she needed was a falling star to wish on, though would one wish be enough to put things right?

But none had fallen by the time Cam returned. He sat beside her, his shoulder warming hers.

It felt so right. She shifted her leg so that it pressed against his from knee to ankle and let out a slow sigh. It *was* right, and yet... As she parted her lips to speak, Cam stirred.

"I talked with Linda, my secretary. The detective I put on Henry Calloway's trail traced him as far as El Paso, then lost him. If he's gone to Mexico, I can kiss that half of my money goodbye."

"I'm sorry."

"Hmph." Cam set two fingers to her back and traced her spine upward. When he reached her hair, he gathered it into one handful and simply held her that way, his knuckles resting against the nape of her neck.

With this simple possession, slow hot waves of pleasure washed through her. *Yes.* "Wh-what about your experts?" she asked unsteadily. "Have they come to any conclusion?"

"Sometime tomorrow, they claim. And Linda can't pry a peep out of 'em as to which way they're leaning."

She could barely hear his sigh, but it echoed her own. "About your money, Cam," she said finally. "I'll find some way to repay it." How many quilts would it take? How many years? Yet it was only right.

He laughed under his breath, and his fingers tightened. "Don't be an idiot, Meek. This is between me and Eli. You'll stay out of it."

"But what will you do?"

Someone's distant lamp painted his hawkish nose in soft gold, tipped his eyelashes with light. Showed her the taut set of his lips. "I don't know," he admitted, his voice low and strained. "It depends. I need to know what he did with all that money. Whether he'll confess..."

But Mr. Finley had said not to let Eli talk with anyone, most of all Cam. And if Eli confessed, why, the lawyer would probably wash his hands of him and his case. Meeka dragged her teeth across her bottom lip.

"You realize, my dear," Cam added huskily, "that if my experts can't prove the letter false, then I'll have to clear George by other means?"

She drew a shaky breath. "What means?"

"A trial. If I charge Eli with fraud, then he'd have to show where he obtained the letter. Since he forged it—can't show he obtained it anywhere—then perhaps I can prove it's false that way, through the back door. And if Eli's convicted of forgery, then George is clearly innocent."

She could hardly swallow. "If you do, Cam..." What kind of an ultimatum could she give him? That she'd take away the love she'd yet to give? He might not laugh in her face—he seemed as blue as she was tonight—but even if he didn't, it wouldn't stop him. Nothing seemed to sway this man from his course. "If you do," she repeated unsteadily. "I'll never speak to you again."

"I know it." His voice was so soft, she could barely hear it.

This is as close as we may ever come, she realized, her tears blurring the starlight. Tonight they could sit here, touching like this, but tomorrow? Tomorrow Eli would come between them. Leaning toward him, she rubbed her nose back and forth against his shoulder. *If this is the only chance I'll ever have, I'll make love with you tonight, Cam. All you have to do is ask.*

But he didn't. He stood abruptly. "Good night, Meek."

The night was anything but.

Sometime toward dawn, she finally found sleep. The next thing she knew, Cam was shaking her shoulder.

"Wake up, Meek. We've overslept."

He looked as tired as she felt, she noticed as they threw together a breakfast of bread, butter, cheese and fruit, then shoved their gear into the car.

Cam checked his watch. "Nearly nine. We'll make it on time."

But the car had other plans—it didn't even wheeze when he turned the key. With a snarl, Cam swung out of the car and lifted the hood. "Alternator, I think," he announced finally. "Whatever, we won't get it going in time." He consulted his watch. "Five miles or so. I can run it in time, Meek, but you'll have to wait here."

"In a pig's eye!" Meeka locked her door. "I'll hitch a ride if I can't keep up with you. I'm sure not staying here."

"And I'm damned if I'll let you hitch a ride by yourself. It's not safe."

"Then come on!"

They jogged perhaps a mile, before she gave out. "It's the hills, not the mileage!" she panted, leaning over to ease a stitch in her side.

"Wait here, then."

"No, I won't." She turned to look back the way they'd come. "Look, here comes somebody." She stopped and stared. A rusty black pickup rumbled uphill. Over its cab, an elegant, furry head surveyed them through arrogant eyes. "It's Jane Rice!"

The truck eased to a halt, and Jane leaned to open the passenger door. "What are you doing here?"

"Car trouble," Meeka said.

"Same as you, I imagine," Cam added. "Did he call you?"

"No, but I can put two and two together, and I got worried. I don't think Eli takes this seriously, or at least, not seriously enough. These people with their guns...and a bounty on his head."

"Could be trouble," Cam agreed. He helped Meeka in, then climbed in beside her. "But why Pizarro?" he asked as the truck groaned into motion.

"Why not?" Jane called over the engine racket. "He goes with me everywhere. And he's a good disarmer. It's hard for people to take themselves too seriously around a llama."

"I'm in Vermont all right," Cam muttered for Meeka's ears. Still, as he leaned back in his seat, he wore a reluctant grin.

They were less than a mile from the muster when Jane slowed the truck. Riding a black mountain bike, a gaunt figure glided downhill, his bony knees and elbows jutting to either side.

"Eli?" Jane muttered.

The man peered into the pickup as he flashed by.

"No!" Meeka cried, turning to look back. "But that's his bike! That's Zundi's basket on back!"

"Get him," Cam commanded. But Jane was already backing and turning.

They chased the rider for nearly a mile before they caught him. Jane sped past the bike, gained some distance, then turned her truck to block both lanes. They scrambled out and moved to block the shoulders.

The biker stopped, stared, then wheeled slowly toward them. "Hey, what is this?" He stopped some twenty feet uphill and frowned, his eyes darting from them to the llama and back again. "What do you want?"

He certainly resembled Eli, Meeka saw now. He was as tall as her uncle and nearly as bony. But he was also thirty years younger.

"We want to know where you got the bike," Cam said immediately. "It belongs to a friend of ours."

"Oh." The man paused, his face reddening. "I didn't steal it, if that's what you think. But I..." He shrugged and set the bike into motion. "I don't think it's any of your business."

"It's very much our business," Cam disagreed, spreading his arms slightly and moving forward to meet the bike. "And we're in a hurry. So where'd you get it and where's the guy you got it from?"

The bike stopped. "He was in a tent at that muster the last I saw of him," the rider said, his face cherry red now. "And I didn't steal his bike, he traded it. He begged me to take it."

"Traded it for what?" Meeka demanded.

The rider hesitated, but Cam moved a step closer, and he spoke hurriedly. "For my costume and the job I was hired to perform. I told him I was getting the best of the bargain. Hawthorne only promised me a hundred for the gig. And the costume's not worth much, though the wig was a pretty good one."

"Gig?" Jane repeated. "You're a musician?"

"An actor," the rider countered. "And a damned good one. Summer stock. And I'm not a bike thief. The old guy said I'd be doing him a favor."

"What's he dressed as?" Cam demanded.

But with a jerk of the handlebars, the actor turned the bike off the road and stood up on the pedals to pump. "Ask him yourself if he's such a friend of yours!" he shouted, as he bumped into the adjoining field and pedaled away. "I promised I wouldn't tell!"

"Damn!" Cam swore. "We'll never catch him now."

"No," Jane said, "but we'll recognize Eli, anyway. At least I will."

The road to the encampment was clogged with spectators' cars, so Jane parked at the bottom of the slope. Cam and Meeka waited while she unloaded Pizarro, but when she led the llama around the truck, she paused. "Oh!" She handed Meeka the llama's lead. "Hold on." Returning to the truck, she pulled a battered brown fedora from behind her seat and put it on. She tilted it to a jaunty angle, then returned to them with a smile. "There!"

"Nice hat," Cam said, his voice soft and expressionless. Meeka glanced at him in alarm, but Jane colored prettily.

"Thanks." She stopped as two children raced up to her, begging to pet the llama.

"I've had that hat for fifteen years," Cam muttered to Meeka, his jaw tight. "It's been with me from Greenland to Nepal to New Zealand and back again."

"Eli gave it to her," Meeka concluded, trapped between delight and dismay. "You couldn't—"

"No, I couldn't," he growled. "But Eli's bill just got bigger."

At the trail up to the camp, four soldiers wearing the black jackets faced with red and the black tricorn hats of the Green Mountain Sons of Liberty stood guard, while a fifth colonial collected admissions. Beside him, a post had been driven into the ground, and Eli's photo grinned from the Wanted poster that had been tacked to it.

"Easy to miss him in this crowd," Cam said as they joined the throng of tourists heading toward the tents. "How tall is he?"

"Six-three," she said, her eyes raking the hillside.

Ka-pow! A puff of smoke rose to one side of the tents where a group of men in uniform had gathered. "The battle starting?" Meeka wondered aloud.

"Target practice." Cam nodded toward a distant square of white.

Ka-pow! The retort echoed off the mountains, and smoke rose again.

"They're using real bullets?" she said worriedly. "But what about during the battle—what happens when they're shooting at each other?"

"They won't." Cam touched her nose when she frowned and started to speak again. "They won't, Meek. He'll be fine. But let's find him before it starts."

They paused to survey the scene. As Meeka watched the men and women moving between the tents, she had a brief odd sensation that it was she who was out of place and time. The soldier who snoozed beside a camp fire, his head propped on a block of wood, looked perfectly at home in this setting. So did the woman in long skirts who stirred a black iron kettle that hung over the fire.

Two fur traders stood by the next tent engaged in fierce negotiation over the trade of a mink pelt for a bear-claw necklace. An Indian girl and her small brother walked a black—

"There!" Cam pointed at the tubby dachshund, tugging at its leash.

"Right shape, wrong color," Meeka reminded him. "Zundi's red."

"Is she? All hot dogs look alike in the dark." Cam turned slowly, surveying the tents. "Is this a reenactment, or a historical flea market?"

Meeka saw what he meant. Every other tent had a Hudson Bay blanket spread before it on which goods were displayed enticingly. One man in a black beaver coat and a dirty felt hat sold tomahawks and vicious-looking knives. At the next blanket, two blond children in Indian garb sold wampum, and two tents down, several Sons of Liberty flirted with a pretty girl dressed in gingham while they purchased paper cartridges and powder horns.

Ka-pow! Meeka jumped. Turning toward the distant musket sound, she saw a familiar face bearing down on them.

"Peterson of the *New York Times!*" the man announced, beaming, as he stopped in front of Cam. Two of his colleagues arrived on his heels, notepads at the ready. "Is it true, Mr. Benson, that your panel of experts will complete their analysis of the George Washington letter today?"

"Nice timing!" added another reporter. "Fourth of July! You will make the results public, won't you, Benson? I'm told that the president is trying to contact you—is that correct? Do you think he hopes to influence the outcome? Maybe ask you to fudge the verdict?"

Meeka ducked between two tents, nearly tripping over the tent pegs in her hurry. Let Cam handle the piranhas if he could. She would look for Eli.

But the newshounds were everywhere. A suave-looking television journalist in a three-piece suit interviewed a tourist, who stared at the camera in dismay, while a crowd gathered to watch. "According to our latest poll, thirty percent of Americans think George did write the so-called George Washington letter," the newsman announced, thrusting his microphone at his target. "What about you, sir? Do you think George was a traitor?"

"W-well," stammered his victim, "I guess. I mean, if you put it like that, thirty percent, well, I always say, where there's smoke, there's fire. I mean, why would there be all this fuss, if there wasn't something to—"

The speaker stopped abruptly as a man in beaded, dazzling white buckskins stepped forth from the crowd. He wore a fox-skin headdress, the fox's muzzle jutting out from his forehead, its glassy-eyed gaze echoing his own. The apparition brandished a hunting knife the size of a small saber. He set the wicked, two-pronged tip of the gleaming implement against the tourist's nose. "Take it back, ya little weasel," he crooned, while the cameraman crowded in at his elbow for a better angle. "Ol' Georgie weren't no lousy traitor, and I'll slit you from your yellow-bellied gizzard to your scrawny gullet if you say he was."

"He *wasn't!*" squeaked the tourist. "Of *course,* he wasn't! I never said—"

"Bliss!" someone said, chortling, in Meeka's ear. "Sheer reportorial bliss."

Meeka turned to find Riley beaming at her. "Such local color!" he added, taking her elbow and guiding her away from the scene.

She stole a glance behind. The tourist had bolted. The TV crew now filmed the mountain man, who, knife upraised, loudly proclaimed George's innocence.

"I thought this would be nothing but Hawthorne's private army, but it's so much more," Riley continued. "The factions are marvelous! There's Hawthorne's continental enlistees—the regular uniformed army, in other words—versus the rough-and-ready militia men who were all volunteers. We've got trappers and traders, both French and American. There's a couple of tepees full of real Indians, and a couple more of wanna-be Indians. Then there's firearm dealers and blanket peddlers and a guy who told me he normally sells discount kitchenware and cosmetics at regular flea markets. He's here selling beaded earrings and colonial soap and straight razors. And there's a horde of camp followers—wives and girlfriends, children and family pets."

Meeka smiled and nodded, and all the while her eyes roamed the crowd. There were many men as tall as Eli here, and the preponderance of hats, from tricorns to red pom-pomed berets to coonskin caps, made it harder to judge their real heights. *Eli could be disguised as just about anything,* she realized. "But you know what's missing?" she asked as they passed an open-air mess hall where some twenty of Justin Hawthorne's Sons of Liberty stood eating stew off tin plates. "There's no redcoats. How is Justin going to throw a revolutionary-war battle without the British?"

Riley smirked. "That's why the delay. Redcoats are hard to come by. Naturally none of your local boys want to play the enemy. So Justin arranged for a troop of reenactors from Toronto to come down and play, er, fight. But apparently their bus has been delayed, and that's a bone of contention."

"Contention?"

"Hawthorne wants to wait for the redcoats' arrival, then stage the thing properly. The fur traders are proposing they stage a skirmish from the French and Indian war instead—French and Indians versus American settlers. The evening-news fellows are siding with the mountain men, since they want to cover the battle, then get back to their stations in time to use it for tonight's Fourth of July broadcast.

"But since their deadlines aren't as pressing, the 'Today Show' and '60 Minutes' would rather wait for the redcoats—a good splash of red versus all this brown and black would really give their footage some zip."

Meeka laughed. "Who's winning?"

"Major Hawthorne, so far. But I'm afraid the mountain men are sulking and the militia are leaning their way, since they can always pretend to be settlers. Hard to keep that old rebellious spirit in line, you know. Most of 'em just want an excuse to shoot guns."

"There you are." Cam dropped an arm around Meeka's shoulders, then frowned at Riley over her head. "Riley."

"Benson." Riley extended his hand. When Cam simply looked at it, he shrugged cheerfully. "Care to place any bets about which way your experts will swing? I hear they're leaning my way."

"Your way?" Meeka repeated.

Riley shrugged again. "If they unanimously declared the letter a blatant forgery, this story would die tomorrow—would be deader than yesterday's fish sticks. But if they think it might be genuine—if even half of 'em vote that way—then, well, there's room for doubt. We could milk this story for weeks. Months!"

"How do you know they're leaning your way?" Cam asked so softly that Riley bent forward to catch the question.

"A scoop from *Scoop!*" he admitted with a wink. Reaching into a pocket, he pulled out a tiny, portable phone. "The same way I'll know your panel's verdict before you do. Shall I let you know when I hear? Should be any time now."

"Don't bother." Cam changed direction abruptly, taking Meeka with him.

Riley made no move to follow, but he called after them, "Meeka? Eli's here, someplace, isn't he?"

She hesitated and looked back, and his smile broadened. "Just remember my offer when you find him," he called before sauntering off the other way.

"His offer?" Cam scowled down at her.

She met his eyes squarely. "Protection from you. Lawyers, money, whatever it takes." *But tell me we don't need it, Cam! Tell me you'll have a heart, and I'll never speak to Riley again.*

"Ah," Cam said, offering no such assurance. His arm dropped away.

Blinking her eyes to fight back the tears, Meeka turned her face away. She blinked again and said, "There's Jane."

Jane and Pizarro stood before a canvas pavilion that was apparently Hawthorne's military headquarters. An American flag and various regimental banners flew before it. Officers came and went with a self-important bustle. And beneath the shade of the canvas, Meeka could make out Hawthorne—Major Hawthorne, in this setting—consulting a map with his lieutenants.

But Jane faced the other way, toward a massive pyramid of wood stacked on the open ground below the tents. "Did you see?" she said as they joined her.

A lumpy scarecrow stood, arms outspread, at the top of the unlit bonfire. But it was Eli's face that grinned back at them. Someone had taped the life-size photo from his Wanted poster to the scarecrow's head. And so that no one would miss the point, a sign hung around the effigy's neck—Eli Trout, Libeler and Traitor.

"I can't stand it!" Jane said furiously. "I tried to take it down, but they stopped me." She nodded at two of Hawthorne's soldiers standing guard below.

"We'll see about that." Cam started downhill, rolling up his sleeves as he went. Meeka and Jane glanced at each other, then hurried after him, Pizarro trotting between them.

"Markus! Kent!" a man's voice yelled from behind them.

"Sir!" The two guards marched past Cam toward their hailer, an officer wearing the red-and-black uniform of a Son of Liberty.

"Form up on the parade ground!" the officer continued. "Inspection in five minutes."

"What's going on?" demanded one of the pair.

"The media are getting restless. So Major Hawthorne's decided that he and General Washington will inspect the troops. Then we burn your buddy." He hooked a thumb at

Eli's effigy. "That'll give the evening-news guys something to film."

"But what about the battle?" the other soldier complained.

The officer shrugged. "Whenever the redcoats get here." He glanced around. "Now, I've got to find that damned actor. Have you seen him?"

The first soldier sniggered. "Hawthorne sure wasted his money on that one! Turns out his General George Washington is a damned injun lover! Last time I saw him, he was in one of the tepees smoking a peace pipe!"

"Well, go drag him out of there!" growled his superior. "Inspection in three minutes." The soldiers hurried off toward the tepees, and the officer marched the other way.

"An actor," Jane said faintly. "Eli wouldn't . . ."

Meeka and Cam glanced at each other. "Oh, yes, he *would!*" As one, they turned and ran.

CHAPTER THIRTEEN

BUT THEY WERE TOO LATE. Meeka and Cam reached the largest of the tepees in time to see six soldiers surround a tall figure wearing the blue beribboned uniform of a general in the Continental Army. "Is that Eli?" Cam hissed.

Meeka stared. Wearing the familiar powdered wig, with that regal bearing and the stern, clean-shaven face, this man could not be her uncle. He was exactly the man he purported to be—General George Washington, father and savior of the country. "I don't think, I mean, I don't see how it could be."

The soldiers formed an honor guard and marched off, George striding in their midst. But he turned back for a last look at his hosts, the crowd of Indians that stood before the tepee, and as he did he dropped them a broad wink. A black dachshund let out a furious yelp and lunged against its leash, which was held by a young girl.

"It's Eli!" Meeka gasped. She'd never seen him without his mustache before, but that wink... and the dog was obviously Zundi with a black rinse. Squaring her shoulders, she started after him.

But Cam caught her arm. "Hold on, my dear. If you try to claim him here and now, what happens? It won't be the scarecrow they burn if they find they have the real Eli. And I'll do my best, but I won't be able to stop them."

"What about the reporters?"

Like a magnet, George Washington and his escort were attracting quite a crowd. Along with tourists and the historical reenactors was a horde of reporters, all following the marching men and drifting toward the open space before the bonfire, where a line of some forty uniformed soldiers stood at parade rest, muskets on shoulders.

Cam snorted. "You think the media will help? They'd love nothing better than bloodshed. Where's Jane?" He glanced around. "We've got to get to her before she blows his cover."

The spectators had formed a dense circle, which straggled up into the tent area, then down and around the parade ground. "You go that way, and I'll go this," Cam said.

It was slow going because the crowd was so thick. Meeka ducked under a camera lens, tripped over children and tent lines while she searched for the llama. She turned to watch the troop inspection as a flourish of drums rolled.

Flanked by two of his aides-de-camp, Major Justin Hawthorne approached Eli—General Washington—with a measured, majestic tread.

What if Hawthorne recognizes him? Meeka wondered, her heart in her mouth. The two men had never been more than nodding acquaintances, and now Eli was clean shaven, but still...

The drums rattled again. Hawthorne smiled a stiff, warrior's smirk and snapped Eli a flawless salute.

Meeka breathed a sigh of relief. The trappings had fooled him, too! No one could see past the wig and the uniform.

Eli returned the salute with the offhand flip of a bored commander-in-chief.

"Atteeeen—Huht!" Hawthorne roared, and the line of soldiers shifted as one. Muskets whirled off shoulders, came to rest smartly, butts down, on the ground alongside each warrior. At one end of the line, about a dozen militiamen tried to match the enlisted men's practiced precision, but fumbled the maneuver. There were chuckles from the crowd, but Hawthorne glared. He leaned close to Eli and sneered something in an undertone.

Jane. Where was Jane? Meeka edged farther around the circle.

"Pre-seeeent arms!" Hawthorne bellowed. Forty palms smacked forty musket stocks. The soldiers raised their weapons before them, muzzles up, forming a jagged fence against the blue sky.

"Quite the performance!" Riley said with a chuckle in Meeka's ear. "And George is the perfect touch. Where did they find him?"

"An actor, I think," Meeka muttered.

"Delicious! And did you see the llama?" Riley nodded across the circle. "My day is complete. A revolutionary-war llama!"

Halfway around the circle, Jane Rice stood in the front row, her hand clenched around Pizarro's halter. Her face was paler than her cloud of silvery hair, and her blue eyes were open wide as she stared straight at Eli.

Oh, Lord, she's going to scream his name right out! Meeka thought.

Instead, the llama trekker jumped violently as a hand closed on her shoulder. Cam wedged his way through the crowd and leaned to say something in her ear.

Meeka glanced nervously at Riley, but he'd missed this interplay. He was frowning at the inspection below. "What's he up to?"

Major Hawthorne and General Washington had reviewed perhaps a third of the troops by now. Eli stopped and said something to a soldier that evoked a startled grin. Hawthorne was starting to frown. Perhaps he hadn't expected such a painstaking inspection from an actor.

"Those guns have got to be getting heavy," Riley observed, and indeed, a few of the out-held muskets were starting to wobble. Eli moved on, stopped short, caught the chin of the Son of Liberty he now faced and scowled ferociously. He turned the man's face left, then right, shook his own head in disgust. Whipping out a handkerchief, he spit on it, scrubbed vigorously at a spot on the man's cheek, then spit on the handkerchief again and scrubbed harder. Then just as quickly, Eli wheeled abruptly and stalked on. Hawthorne simply stared after him, then recovering with a jerk, hurried to catch up.

"And what's going on over there?" Riley asked.

Following his gaze, Meeka looked downhill past the bonfire. A group of perhaps a dozen fur traders and mountain men was sauntering with exaggerated casualness along the brow of the hill. But their formation was all wrong. They huddled against each other, elbows jostling, as if—

"They're hiding something!" Riley muttered, standing on tiptoe to see. "What's that behind them? A cannon?"

Someone stumbled and Meeka caught a glimpse of a wide cart wheel and a dark, tubular shape before the gap closed. The band of men shuffled down the slope and vanished below the rim of the hill.

"Strange," Riley mused. He scanned the crowd, and his eyes narrowed. "Come to think of it, where are the rest of the trappers and traders?"

Meeka glanced around. With all the tourists, reporters, and settlers in view, it didn't seem possible that anyone could be missing. Yet, now that Riley mentioned it... "And Indians," she added. "There were Indians here when this started, weren't there?"

"Powwow back at the tepees perhaps," Riley suggested. "Who wants to watch an inspection, anyway?"

"Sloppy, soldier! Pretty sloppy!" a familiar voice roared.

There were less than a dozen men left to inspect. Eli had fastened on one and was tugging at the luckless soldier's uniform jacket.

"Misbuttoned it?" Riley wondered aloud just as the two sides of the jacket came apart with a familiar ripping noise.

"Velcro!" Eli yelled, glaring at the jacket's fastening. "You use Velcro? This is the American Revolution, soldier! What are you doing with Velcro?"

Behind him, Hawthorne's mouth gaped, closed soundlessly, then gaped again. Eli released his victim and stalked to the next. Catching him by the collar, he yanked.

Riip! The jacket peeled open, exposing a white jerkin and a beer belly.

"His is Velcro, too! This is a disgrace!" Storming down the line, Eli wrenched open jacket after jacket as he went. "Velcro at Valley Forge! The Brits would have heard us coming!" *Riip.*

"Velcro at the Battle of Bunker Hill—they'd have laughed us right out of town! *Riip.* Not a historically correct honest bone button among you, you lily-livered, sons of—"

The crowd's hysterical laughter drowned him out. "I thought you said he was shy?" Cam demanded. In the growing confusion, he, Jane and her llama had simply cut across the edge of the circle. "Is he nuts?"

"No, he's mad—fighting mad," Jane asserted. "How would you like to be chased around the country and vilified? Burned in effigy?"

Riley stared from Jane to Cam to Meeka, then swung his gaze to the mounting uproar below. "You mean *that's*—"

"You, too?" Eli bellowed. To Hawthorne's patent relief, he'd come to the end of the line. But instead of concluding his inspection, he'd turned and caught the major by his collar. *"Et tu, Brute?"* He didn't wait for an answer. *Riip.* Hawthorne's immaculate uniform gaped wide. "Velcro City! I'm going back to Mount Vernon, and a pox on you all! You can find some other sucker for president!"

"What are you, *crazy?*" Hawthorne howled, struggling to close his uniform.

Eli shook his head, then said something in a voice pitched only for the major's ears.

Eyes bugging, Hawthorne rocked back on his heels.

Eli nodded cheerfully, bowed, doffed his powdered wig in a sweeping salute—then plopped it on Hawthorne's head. He turned and walked away.

"That's Eli *Trout!*" Hawthorne screamed, clawing the wig off. "That's the traitor who libeled George Washington!" He brandished the wig after him. "Get him, boys!"

And that's when the battle began.

Ka-pow! Ka-pow! Ka-pow! A dozen muskets cracked from the edges of the forest. The spectators wheeled around as a hair-raising Indian war cry sounded from above. A woman screamed. A woman in calicos came running between the tents, screaming as she came, and a female tourist beside Meeka echoed the scream wholeheartedly.

"French and Indian war won out!" Riley concluded blissfully as another musket volley let loose. "Who needs the British?"

Racing out of the woods, the raiders darted from tent to tent, driving the long-skirted women and gleefully shrieking children before them as they came. Tourists yelped, fled or paused to take photographs. Cameramen and reporters dashed toward the action. The male settlers drew knives and tomahawks or ran for their guns, while out on the parade ground half of Hawthorne's soldiers had rallied to form disciplined ranks and were waiting for the command to fire.

But Hawthorne wasn't commanding them.

"Eli! Where's Eli?" Meeka yelled.

Riley pointed. Eli was just rounding the far side of the bonfire with Justin Hawthorne and a dozen soldiers hot on his heels. Behind them, Cam paused to wrench a musket from the hands of a startled soldier. Then, running with long, lithe strides, he, too, vanished in their wake.

Ka-pow! The soldiers got off an impressive volley. White smoke billowed. With a howl, a man in buckskin, a French stocking cap and red war paint rolled over and over to land at Meeka's feet. His feet kicked the ground in a pattering convulsion, then he lay still.

He sat up almost immediately and began to reload his musket.

"You're dead," Riley pointed out.

"*Oui,* but that's no fun," the trapper said cheerfully. Ramming down a charge, he leapt to his feet and darted away, whooping.

Meanwhile, Jane had her hands full as her llama spun in a crazed and bucketing circle. The cameraman from "60 Minutes" stopped to film her for a moment, then turned to chase a settler woman who held her skirts high with one hand while she brandished a knife with the other. The woman leapt lightly over a tent rope and vanished. Eye to his viewfinder, the cameraman blundered into the same rope and vanished—horizontally.

Meeka winced. Eli—where was Eli—and Cam? Heading after them, she tore past the bonfire. Two children in coonskin caps knelt beside it. One appeared to be striking sparks with a flint and steel, while the other blew gently on a pile of wood chips.

Out on the small plain beyond the bonfire, the battle raged. The only pattern in the chaos was the band of soldiers who'd rallied around Justin Hawthorne. Shoulder to shoulder, they advanced grimly against an opposing force in buckskin—the Indians, real and counterfeit. And—"*Cam!*" she cried.

But he couldn't hear her. Looking fierce enough to let real blood, he whirled his musket, stock first, holding off two advancing soldiers. Just beyond him, George Washington—Eli—shook a tomahawk at his pursuers and whooped in defiance.

"Looks like the army's winning," Riley observed, catching up with her. "Do you think they'll hurt him?" he added hopefully.

Meeka glared at him, then gaped as he stopped, whipped his portable telephone out of his pocket and put it to his ear. "Yes?"

A blond-haired Indian woman, racing toward her comrades, paused to rap Riley on the head with a tomahawk. He glanced up at her in a moment of pure shock, then grinned and sank obediently to his knees. Collapsing on his side, he continued to talk on the phone.

"That's the traitor!" Hawthorne roared, pointing at Eli. "I want him alive!" He'd rallied twenty Sons of Liberty to his cause, and they were overwhelming Eli's defenders. Meeka looked around for a weapon. Everyone else might be playing, but Hawthorne was not, she was sure.

That was when the cannon was wheeled up the rise and into view. A crew of grinning mountain men in beaver coats, led by the fox-headed swashbuckler in beaded white buckskin, aimed their surprise weapon at Hawthorne's troops.

"Ready," he yelled. "Aim."

The Sons of Liberty stopped, stared over their shoulders in dismay, then turned to face the artillery.

"Forget about that!" howled Hawthorne. "It's the traitor Trout, we—"

"Fire!" yelled the man in white buckskin.

Boom! Meeka clapped her hands over her ears as a cloud of smoke belched from the cannon's mouth.

Bowing to superior special effects, Hawthorne's men collapsed in various poses of kicking mortality.

"Get up, you idiots!" Hawthorne yelled, standing all alone.

"Retreat!" yelled a very large and genuine-looking Indian chief who stood next to Cam. "Friends of Washington, back to the tepees!"

Cam's eyes picked Meeka out of the melee. "Move it, my dear!" he yelled, his grin very white in a face darkened by gunpowder. His hands were full, one grasping his musket, the other holding up Eli, who now sported a very real-looking stripe of blood across his forehead. Cam jerked his chin toward the tepees, and Meeka needed no further invitation.

The soldiers were beginning to rise from the dead, as Hawthorne berated them, and the Indians were quickly dispersing. Meeka grabbed an abandoned musket and ran.

Weapons drawn, a ring of Indians—some apparently genuine, some Indian only by virtue of their feathers and war paint—stood with their backs to the largest tepee. Cam waited for Meeka by the entrance. Taking her musket, he handed it to a tall brave. "This is the last one we want inside," he said. "See if you can hold 'em off." He nodded toward Hawthorne's advancing troops.

Apparently some sort of truce had been effected. This grim-faced contingent now included several mountain men, and in their midst rolled—

"A cannon?" Cam's comrade looked doubtful. "This may be Custer's last stand—in reverse!"

"Do your best." Cam pulled Meeka into the tepee.

She paused, blinking in the dim light, which came mainly from a smoke hole overhead. Then she made out Eli seated on the far side of the circle of warriors. A woman in buckskin was tying a rag bandage around his forehead. "Eli!" Meeka threw herself at him.

"Meek!" Beaming, he hugged her. "So you got my postcard?"

"Yes, you goof! But I didn't bring you a ham sandwich." She tried unsuccessfully to fend off the black dachshund that had climbed into her lap and was now kissing her enthusiastically. "You neither, Gezundheit." She laughed, wiping her mouth.

"That's okay." Eli gestured around the circle. "We met up with these kind people last night and they fed us. We were mighty famished."

"To put it mildly!" chuckled one of the Indians. "We named him Chief Eat a Horse. And that," he nodded at Zundi, "is Long Pig."

"But I did bring someone to meet you," Meeka added, leaning back so that Eli could see Cam, who had settled, cross-legged, on her other side.

"Oh—" Eli grinned and reached past her to shake his hand "—we've already met. This guy saved my hide out there. That damn Hawthorne never could take a joke."

"What I didn't have time to tell you is that I'm Cameron Benson," Cam said wryly. "My magazine bought your letter."

"That's where I've seen you before!" Eli's grin widened. "You're the young fella in the tent, at the carnival! You own *American Historic?*"

"I do." Cam didn't return his grin. "But I don't believe for a minute that George Washington was ever a traitor."

"Uh..." Across the tepee, someone cleared his throat. One of the outside guards stood by the entrance. "I've got a guy out here says he has a phone call for Chief Eat a Horse." He jerked a thumb at Riley, who had pushed into the tepee behind him.

Riley's eyes scanned the circle of upturned faces, then he smiled and crossed to Eli, his portable phone extended. "Mr. Trout?" He handed Eli the phone. "No phone call, really. That was just an excuse so I could meet you."

"Oh. Glad to meet you." Eli set the phone down between Zundi's paws and turned back to Benson. "You were saying?"

Riley shrugged and sat with his back to the central fire. He reached for his phone, then stopped when Zundi curled her lip in a soundless snarl. He shrugged and sat back again.

"I was saying that I'm convinced the letter is a forgery, presumably forged by you," Cam continued. "I mean to publish a retraction in my next issue. To make it absolutely irrefutable, I want to publish your confession. Why you wrote the letter. How you wrote it."

"Wait!" Riley cried as Eli started to speak. "Before you say anything, Mr. Trout, you should know this. A panel of the world's most renowned document experts has just declared the George Washington letter to be *absolutely authentic.* They say there's no doubt at all that it's written on paper of the period, with the proper ink, in George Washington's own hand."

Eli laughed with delight. "They do? The world's top experts?"

"They do." Riley nodded vigorously. "And so, on behalf of *Scoop,* I'd like to offer you $10,000 for your exclusive story on how and where you obtained the letter that proves George Washington's treachery."

A buzz of reaction circled the tepee when Riley named the sum. Meeka stole a worried glance at Cam. His jaw muscles stood out in sharply cut and shifting relief.

"And of course we'll take care of any and all court costs," Riley added smoothly, avoiding Cam's glare, "should anyone be so foolish as to trouble you. All we ask in return is your story, which I'd, ahem, be delighted to help you write."

"Ten thousand dollars!" Eli repeated, his bushy eyebrows waggling with amusement.

Meeka caught his arm. "Eli, first there's something you should know about Cam and— Ow!" she yelped as someone pinched her thigh. She turned to glare at Cam.

Unrepentant, he put a forefinger to her nose. "Meeka, stay out of this," he warned. "Let him make up his own mind."

"So Mr. Riley's offering me $10,000 to keep on with the gag," Eli mused. "And what are you offering, Benson?"

Cam's voice was very low and bleakly courteous. "You have one hundred thousand of mine already, Trout. I'm not offering a red cent more."

"Not a red cent?" Eli rubbed his chin and looked down at Zundi, who tipped her long nose to stare back at him. "What do you think, Gezundheit?"

Everyone in the tepee leaned forward as man and dog consulted. Finally Eli nodded, satisfied. "Deal," he said, turning to Cam. "Of course George Washington never did it. And if everybody's going to make such a fuss about it," he added, raising his voice over the mounting exclamations, "then I might as well tell the truth."

Cam let out a heartfelt sigh of relief. "You forged the letter," he clarified, while he slipped a hand around Meeka's arm and squeezed.

"I forged it," Eli agreed. "And you've got to admit I did a damned fine job of it! But I never meant to send it to you. It was supposed to be a private joke—between me and Hawthorne." He glanced across the tepee to where another Indian had slipped inside and was conferring earnestly with the chief. "Speaking of which," he called, "how's Hawthorne doing out there? Is he all set to blow us to kingdom come?"

"He was working up to it," the chief confirmed. "But somebody lit the bonfire, and now '60 Minutes' wants to film his side of the story in front of your burning effigy, and that's kind of distracted him."

"We'll need to start writing your story today," Cam said, returning to his own concerns. "I'm not waiting for my usual deadline. I want the issue out on the street as soon as possible."

"Wait!" Riley spread his arms wide, his palms up. "Now wait just a minute." He turned to Cam. "You're wasting the opportunity of a lifetime, and there's no need for it! Everybody can win here."

Cam smiled and shook his head.

"They can!" Riley insisted. "Just think a minute. This story is worth millions if we spin it out! With your own experts testifying that the letter is genuine, we could drag out the debate for weeks. Your next issue would sell out—you could double your usual price, and quadruple your print run, for that matter. And *Scoop* could sell to the lowbrow market while you take the high, no problem there. And there might even be room for a three-way collaboration here—a book. What do you think about that?"

"I think everybody in this tepee already knows the truth about George," Cam said, his voice very dry.

"No problem," Riley insisted. His eyes swept the circle. "A thousand bucks for each of you gentlemen," he said, "to keep it under your, er, hats for three months." He raised his voice to be heard over the rumble this offer elicited. "And at the end of three months, why, we simply reverse ourselves. Just when everybody is finally convinced that George is a traitor and they're heartily sick of it all, we print Mr. Trout's confession—and we sell out all over again! That's the beauty of it. We scoop 'em coming and going, and where's the harm?"

"Where's the harm?" Cam repeated softly. "If you can't see it, I can't even begin to tell you. So just be quiet and sit—"

"But—"

"Sit...*still,*" Cam almost whispered. "Or so help me..." He jerked his head, shaking some thought aside, and turned back to Eli. "There's just one more point, Mr. Trout, but it's a very important one."

Meeka had been anticipating this. "Cam, I'll pay back your hundred thousand! I really will, if you'll just let me work out some sort of installment—"

Cam clapped a hand over her mouth. "The point is," he continued serenely, "that I intend to marry your niece." He took his hand away and glanced at her, his eyebrows angled.

Meeka's jaw slowly dropped. *Marriage!* She'd prayed for some sort of chance to get to know him, now that Eli didn't stand between them, but—

Cam leaned forward and kissed her, and she laughed against his lips. Dimly she could hear cheers and sounds of male approval. When at last he let her go, her cheeks were burning, but she looked around at Eli with shining eyes.

Eli looked neither surprised nor displeased. In fact, he was solemnly shaking Zundi's paw, as if they'd planned it all between them. But then he looked up again, frowning. "What's this about your hundred thousand?"

"Forget it," Cam said quickly. "It would have been nice to recover it, but consider it a bride price." The arm he'd slipped around Meeka tightened. "I got the best of the bargain."

Eli looked puzzled. "I mailed that back to you ages ago—the day I cashed the check. You mean to say you never got it? A shoe box full of money? I called your magazine, got the address and mailed it there."

"Then it's..." Cam started to laugh. "It's probably still there in my office. My secretary tells me we've been receiving about a ton of mail a day since we published your letter. I imagine it's at the bottom of the pile."

"But why did you ever cash the check?" Meeka wanted to know. Not that she really cared. Now everything was complete. Cam wouldn't think Eli was a thief, and she...she and Cam...

"Wanted to see the look on Hilda May's face when I asked for a hundred thousand dollars in unmarked, used singles," Eli said reasonably. "How could I resist?"

Their messenger to the outside world had returned, and now he cleared his throat. "There's a lady with a llama out here, says if you don't let Eli out, she and her llama are coming in after him. And there's about half a hundred damned reporters who'd be happy to give her a hand."

"Jane?" Eli said wonderingly.

Meeka looked quickly at his face, and his shy, fleeting smile told her all she needed to know.

"Jane?" Eli murmured again as he stood and tugged at his uniform. He glanced down, stooped to brush some imagined dust off of Zundi's hide, then turned toward the exit. But he paused and glanced back at Cam. "What do we tell all those news fellas out there?"

"We tell them the truth—the sooner the better." Cam rose to his feet, then gave Meeka his hand. Lifting her up, he caught her by her upper arms and pulled her close. "That was a proposal back there, but I didn't hear a yes," he said, his voice low and fierce.

"Yes!" she replied, leaning against him.

His fingers tightened as he searched her eyes. "Just like that? No conditions, no what-about-Eli?"

"No conditions—" she laughed "—except always and forever, and one four-poster bed."

"Deal!" he said so softly no one else could hear. They sealed it with a kiss, then followed Eli out into sunlight, to face the waiting crowd.

Where do you find hot Texas nights, smooth Texas charm and dangerously sexy cowboys?

Crystal Creek reverberates with the exciting rhythm of Texas. Each story features the rugged individuals who live and love in the Lone Star state.

"...Crystal Creek wonderfully evokes the hot days and steamy nights of a small Texas community...impossible to put down until the last page is turned."
—*Romantic Times*

"...a series that should hook any romance reader. Outstanding."
—*Rendezvous*

"Altogether, it couldn't be better." —*Rendezvous*

Don't miss the next book in this exciting series:
LET'S TURN BACK THE YEARS by BARBARA KAYE

Available in August wherever Harlequin books are sold.

INDULGE A LITTLE 6947 SWEEPSTAKES
NO PURCHASE NECESSARY

HERE'S HOW THE SWEEPSTAKES WORKS:
The Harlequin Reader Service shipments for January, February and March 1994 will contain, respectively, coupons for entry into three prize drawings: a trip for two to San Francisco, an Alaskan cruise for two and a trip for two to Hawaii. To be eligible for any drawing using an Entry Coupon, simply complete and mail according to directions.

There is no obligation to continue as a Reader Service subscriber to enter and be eligible for any prize drawing. You may also enter any drawing by hand printing your name and address on a 3" x 5" card and the destination of the prize you wish that entry to be considered for (i.e., San Francisco trip, Alaskan cruise or Hawaiian trip). Send your 3" x 5" entries to: Indulge a Little 6947 Sweepstakes, c/o Prize Destination you wish that entry to be considered for, P.O. Box 1315, Buffalo, NY 14269-1315, U.S.A. or Indulge a Little 6947 Sweepstakes, P.O. Box 610, Fort Erie, Ontario L2A 5X3, Canada.

To be eligible for the San Francisco trip, entries must be received by 4/30/94; for the Alaskan cruise, 5/31/94; and the Hawaiian trip, 6/30/94. No responsibility is assumed for lost, late or misdirected mail. Sweepstakes open to residents of the U.S. (except Puerto Rico) and Canada, 18 years of age or older. All applicable laws and regulations apply. Sweepstakes void wherever prohibited.

For a copy of the Official Rules, send a self-addressed, stamped envelope (WA residents need not affix return postage) to: Indulge a Little 6947 Rules, P.O. Box 4631, Blair, NE 68009, U.S.A.

INDR93

INDULGE A LITTLE 6947 SWEEPSTAKES
NO PURCHASE NECESSARY

HERE'S HOW THE SWEEPSTAKES WORKS:
The Harlequin Reader Service shipments for January, February and March 1994 will contain, respectively, coupons for entry into three prize drawings: a trip for two to San Francisco, an Alaskan cruise for two and a trip for two to Hawaii. To be eligible for any drawing using an Entry Coupon, simply complete and mail according to directions.

There is no obligation to continue as a Reader Service subscriber to enter and be eligible for any prize drawing. You may also enter any drawing by hand printing your name and address on a 3" x 5" card and the destination of the prize you wish that entry to be considered for (i.e., San Francisco trip, Alaskan cruise or Hawaiian trip). Send your 3" x 5" entries to: Indulge a Little 6947 Sweepstakes, c/o Prize Destination you wish that entry to be considered for, P.O. Box 1315, Buffalo, NY 14269-1315, U.S.A. or Indulge a Little 6947 Sweepstakes, P.O. Box 610, Fort Erie, Ontario L2A 5X3, Canada.

To be eligible for the San Francisco trip, entries must be received by 4/30/94; for the Alaskan cruise, 5/31/94; and the Hawaiian trip, 6/30/94. No responsibility is assumed for lost, late or misdirected mail. Sweepstakes open to residents of the U.S. (except Puerto Rico) and Canada, 18 years of age or older. All applicable laws and regulations apply. Sweepstakes void wherever prohibited.

For a copy of the Official Rules, send a self-addressed, stamped envelope (WA residents need not affix return postage) to: Indulge a Little 6947 Rules, P.O. Box 4631, Blair, NE 68009, U.S.A.

INDR93

INDULGE A LITTLE SWEEPSTAKES

OFFICIAL ENTRY COUPON

This entry must be received by: JUNE 30, 1994
This month's winner will be notified by: JULY 15, 1994
Trip must be taken between: AUGUST 31, 1994-AUGUST 31, 1995

YES, I want to win the 3-Island Hawaiian vacation for two. I understand that the prize includes round-trip airfare, first-class hotels and pocket money as revealed on the "wallet" scratch-off card.

Name____

Address ________________________ Apt. ____________

City____

State/Prov.__________________ Zip/Postal Code____________

Daytime phone number________________________________
(Area Code)

Account #____

Return entries with invoice in envelope provided. Each book in this shipment has two entry coupons—and the more coupons you enter, the better your chances of winning!

 MONTH3

INDULGE A LITTLE SWEEPSTAKES

OFFICIAL ENTRY COUPON

This entry must be received by: JUNE 30, 1994
This month's winner will be notified by: JULY 15, 1994
Trip must be taken between: AUGUST 31, 1994-AUGUST 31, 1995

YES, I want to win the 3-Island Hawaiian vacation for two. I understand that the prize includes round-trip airfare, first-class hotels and pocket money as revealed on the "wallet" scratch-off card.

Name____

Address ________________________ Apt. ____________

City____

State/Prov.__________________ Zip/Postal Code____________

Daytime phone number________________________________
(Area Code)

Account #____

Return entries with invoice in envelope provided. Each book in this shipment has two entry coupons—and the more coupons you enter, the better your chances of winning!

© 1993 HARLEQUIN ENTERPRISES LTD. MONTH3